SKERRY TALES

MILTON J. DAVIS

MVmedia, LLC
Fayetteville, GA

MVmedia, LLC
PO Box 143052
Fayetteville, GA 30215
info@mvmediaatl.com
www.mvmediaatl.com

Cover art by Oz Ezeogu
Cover design by URAEUS

Publisher's Note: This is a work of fiction. Names, characters, places, and incidents are a product of the author's imagination. Locales and public names are sometimes used for atmospheric purposes. Any resemblance to actual people, living or dead, or to businesses, companies, events, institutions, or locales is completely coincidental.

Ordering Information:
Quantity sales. Special discounts are available on quantity purchases by corporations, associations, and others. For details, contact the "Special Sales Department" at the address above.

Skerry Tales/ Milton J. Davis. -- 1st ed.
ISBN 979-8-9905121-3-9

CONTENTS

I ain't skerd.

—Unknown

Betta Listen

The house wasn't much but it was all he could afford. Stephanie told him a hundred times they needed more life insurance, but he didn't listen. Life insurance was for old people; they were still in their thirties and in great shape. Nothing could or would happen to them.

Randolph Chambers followed the moving truck up the steep driveway then thought better of it. They would need room to take out the furniture, what little there was. Steph's chemo drained everything they had and then some. What little he was able to keep was augmented by donations from family and friends. They should have counted themselves lucky, but they didn't. Randolph would rather be homeless with Steph and Gina than alone in a mansion.

"So, this is home now?" Gina barely looked up from her cellphone. It was their last luxury, a gift from a co-worker.

"Yeah, baby girl, this is home."

"Unh huh." Randolph heard her shift in her seat, but he didn't look at her. It was hard for him to. He hated to see the disappointment in her face and the pain that lingered just beneath it. She looked so much like her mother, her gestures and expressions a reflection of Stephanie. He gathered himself and turned to her, forcing a smile on his face.

"Come on. Let's see what our little bit of money bought us."

He parked the SUV next to the curb and exited. He was halfway up the driveway when he noticed Gina was still in the vehicle. He walked back and tapped on her window. She looked at him, raising her eyebrows in annoyance.

"Roll down the window," he said.

The window slid down.

"Aren't you coming?"

Gina rolled her eyes and snatched her earphones off her head. "It's just a house. It's not home."

Randolph ignored the insult, just as he'd done every day since Stephanie died. The psychiatrist said it was normal for children to act out after a parent's death, so he sucked it in and took the blows. Some days it was harder than others.

Gina finally climbed out and they trudged up the driveway and into the house. Randolph had hoped his opinion of the modest home would change after a few weeks, but it didn't. He should have been thankful to be in a house at all, but he wasn't. Everything was less now.

He forced a smile. "Why don't you go pick out your room?"

Gina stared at the floor. "It doesn't matter."

"Well pick out mine then."

Gina cut him a curious glance. "Sure, whatever." She stomped up the stairs.

Randolph stepped aside as the movers brought in the great room furniture and sat it down in the room to his right. He went down the narrow hallway into the kitchen/dinette area and did a quick inspection. He'd have to replace the faucets when he got paid. The laundry room was a cramped space that barely accommodated the stacked washer and dryer, but it would do.

"Daddy!"

Randolph broke his musing and trotted upstairs. "What's up, baby girl?"

"I'm in here."

Randolph entered the first room. Gina sat on the floor in the corner, a serious look on her face.

"This is it. This is my room."

Randolph looked about the empty space and frowned. It was the smallest room in the house; her furniture wouldn't fit. He'd have to put her chest of drawers in another room or the basement.

"You sure you want this . . ."

"I'm sure. This is my room."

Randolph shrugged and walked out. He knew it wasn't the right response, but he didn't care. He was tired, physically, and mentally. He'd be a better father tomorrow.

He spent the next three hours leading the movers around the house making sure everything was in its proper place. He wouldn't have much help arranging furniture once the movers left. Most of his friends were really Stephanie's friends. After the mandatory support period they all slowly disappeared. His real friends lived in his hometown of Atlanta, too far away to drop by and lend a hand. Stacy Upchurch, his best friend, had

promised to fly out to visit 'as soon as he got settled,' but Stacy was never settled.

The movers arranged Gina's furniture around
her. She sat in the corner of the room, eyes closed
and head bobbing to whatever played on her cellphone.

"Where do you want your bed?" he asked.

"I don't care," Gina replied.

"Set it by the window," Randolph told the
movers.

"No!" Gina jumped to her feet, her expression
angry. "Anywhere but there."

Randolph had enough. "Take off those damn
earphones!"

Gina glared at him then removed them.

Randolph folded his arms. "Now you're going
to tell these hard-working men where you want
your furniture and you're going to do it politely.
And if you snap at me one more time, I'm going
to snatch that cellphone and throw it into the
street. You understand?"

Gina nodded her head.

"Do you understand?"

Gina looked away. "Yes, sir."

Randolph stormed out of the room. When the
movers were done, he gave them a generous tip
then went to his own room. He'd sold the king
size bed and replaced it with a queen. The king
was too big, but that wasn't the reason he sold it.
Stephanie loved that bed with its tall rice posts,
standing so high from the floor she needed a step
stool to climb into it. She used to say it made her
feel like a child to sit on it, her feet dangling over

the edge. The bed even smelled like her, or at least her favorite perfume. When he slept in the old bed her memories awakened. So he sold it not because he wanted to, but because he had to. That was when things between him and Gina started going bad. She accused him of trying to forget Stephanie. He couldn't get her to understand that he wasn't trying to forget. He just couldn't have her memories so close.

The good thing about the new/old house was that it was still in Gina's school district. The bad thing was that Randolph had to drive her to school. It wouldn't have been a problem before. He was a street salesman before Stephanie took ill and he could arrange his calls around his personal life. Once Stephanie was diagnosed, he took an inside sales position. It was less money and he hated sitting at a desk all day, but he needed to be close to make sure she made her treatments and to help around the house. Having to take Gina to school meant getting up earlier, and Randolph was not a morning person. But that didn't matter.

* * *

"Breakfast is ready!" Randolph yelled.

Gina stomped down the hallway and dropped into her chair. Randolph did a finishing flourish with the scrambled eggs then slid a portion on her plate. He scooped a spoonful of grits beside the eggs then placed two pieces of bacon on the edge.

"Good morning," he said.

"Yeah," Gina replied. Randolph would have been shocked if she had said more. She attacked the food like a starving child as he made his own plate and sat opposite her.

"So how was your first night in the new room?"

"Terrible," she mumbled.

Randolph nodded. "The first night in a new house can be rough."

"It was all that damn noise."

Randolph mixed his eggs and grits. "What noise?"

"All that talking. I guess it was the neighbors. You didn't hear it?"

"No." Randolph glanced at the clock. "Shit...I mean Darn it. It's almost time to go. Hurry up."

"I just got here!" Gina whined.

"It's either ride or walk," Randolph retorted.

Gina scooped up her food. "You need to talk to the neighbors. They're too loud."

She sounded like Stephanie. "I will. Now let's get you to school and me to work."

Randolph sped to the school and joined the parent processional. He was two cars away from the drop off point when Tanisha Bridges came outside. The young pretty assistant principal came straight for their car.

"Not today," Randolph whispered. "I don't have time for this."

She walked up to the passenger door, flashing her bright smile and waving as if they were a mile away. Gina opened the door and stepped onto the curb. She was immediately swallowed into Tanisha's hug.

"Welcome back, Gina! We missed you!"

"Yeah," Gina replied. She escaped Tanisha's embrace and trudged to the school building.

Tanisha turned her attention to Randolph.

"How is everything, Randolph?" she asked with over exaggerated concern.

"As good as can be expected," Randolph replied.

"These things take time, Randolph. Is it okay if I call you Randolph?"

Hell no!

"It's fine, Ms. Bridges."

"Please, call me Tanisha."

The tenor of her smile changed, its intention matching her words.

"I'd love to talk" —why did he say that — "but I'm late for work." Randolph shifted the SUV into drive.

"I understand Randolph. We'll talk soon." She closed the door and waved, mouthing the words, *"Have a nice day."*

Randolph crept to the stoplight at the entrance of the school then into traffic. Steph was right. Ms. Barnes —Tanisha— did have a crush on him. She would tease him during PTO meetings about how Tanisha would look him up and down and giggle like a twelve-year-old whenever he said something witty. It was funny then, but not now. Now she seemed like a vulture, waiting to swoop down on the remains of their marriage. He debated whether to curse her out the next time he saw her.

He pulled into the parking lot ten minutes late. As he snuck into the side entrance he encountered Taylor Freemen, his boss, standing before the coffee dispenser filling his cup. He cut an eye at Randolph then at the break room clock.

"Morning, Randy," he said coolly.

"Good morning."

Randolph hurried by him. He went directly to his cubicle and sat in front of his computer. He was logging in when Taylor appeared over him.

"How's it going?" he asked.

"Fine,"

"How's Gina doing?"

"Fine."

"Is there anything I can do?"

"No."

Taylor lingered and the moment became awkward. Randolph waited for him to say it. Taylor wasn't a tactful man, so his hesitance was out of character. He's seen his boss rake other employees over the coals for taking too much bereavement time. But Randolph was different. He'd been the company's best salesman when he was on the road and now, he was its best in-house sale rep. Firing him meant losing money and Taylor hated losing money. It wasn't that Randolph's work was bad; he was still closing deals head over heels compared to the other reps, he just wasn't producing Randolph numbers.

Taylor scratched his balding head. "Well, if you need to talk or anything, let me know. We're

. . . I mean I'm here to help. You're a valuable employee and I know things are tough right now. We want to see you back to your old self."

"So I can get back to making you money."

"Sure, thanks Taylor. I really appreciate it."

Randolph logged in and went through the motions of the day. On his worst day he was better than most, and the past few weeks were his worst days. Before Steph's illness he was road warrior, a street salesman bouncing from city to city and sometimes state to state hawking TF's electronic goods. But he requested an inside job when she was diagnosed. Upper management resisted until he threatened to quit.

He ate lunch at his desk. On his screen a string of memories scrolled by, images of his life during better times. Photos of Hilton Head spring vacations, summers in Canada and winters in Miami marched by in perfect time, triggering as much joy as pain. He watched the images parade by repeatedly. He was still watching them when his phone rang. It was going to be another wasted day.

"Hello?" His voice was almost angry when he answered.

"Randolph, this is Tanisha. We need you to come to the school immediately. There's an issue with Gina."

"I'll be right there." Randolph hung up the phone before Tanisha could explain. He grabbed his things and rushed toward the door.

"Hey, hey hold up partner!" Taylor yelled. "Where are you running to? You just got here."

"Trouble at my daughter's school," Randolph shouted back. "I'll be in early tomorrow."

He sped to the school. Tanisha waited outside. "What's going on, Tanisha?"

"Gina was in a fight."

"Fight? Gina's never been in a fight in her life! What happened? Was someone picking on her? You know she's…"

"Calm down, Randolph." Tanisha placed a comforting hand on his shoulder. He flinched then cut his eyes at Tanisha. She took her hand away.

"Gina started the fight. She's in the principal's office right now. As much as I hate it, we have to suspend her for two days."

Randolph nodded absently. "I understand."

"Will there be anyone at home with her?"

"I'll take the days off," he said immediately, knowing he'd catch hell from Taylor. "I'll figure out some way to work from home."

Tanisha nodded then walked away. "Follow me."

Randolph trailed Tanisha through the narrow halls to the principal's office. Gina sat by the door. Her clothes were crumpled, and a dark bruise formed around her left eye. He knelt in front of her.

"You alright, baby girl?"

Gina nodded. "Don't call me that."

"Mr. Chambers?"

Randolph turned to see Principal Wiggins approaching him. He shook the principal's hand, wincing as the tall ex-football player squeezed a bit too hard.

"I'm sorry we have to meet under such circumstances," Wiggins said. "Gina's usually a good young lady. This is as much a surprise to us, as I'm sure it is to you."

"It is," Randolph said. He was angry and embarrassed.

"I wish we could manage this situation differently due to Gina's circumstances, but rules are rules. We have to suspend her."

Gina's circumstances? So, Stephanie's death was just circumstances to them.

"As I told Ms. Bridges, I understand."

He went back to Gina. "Come on, let's go."

Gina followed him to the SUV. They rode home in silence. Randolph didn't know what to say. He was angry at her for fighting, but he knew it had something to do with Stephanie. She should be punished, but how would she take it? He couldn't do it any longer. It was time to talk to a therapist. No matter how he tried he couldn't make it right on his own. The pain went deep like old roots.

He was still coming to a stop when Gina flung open the car door then jumped out. She was fumbling with her keys at the door by the time he exited the car.

"Gina?"

She shoved open the door then went inside. Randolph followed her to her room. When he entered, she was on the bed crying. He tried to speak to her, searching his mind for a string of comforting words to say but he came up empty. The truth was he wanted to do the same thing, but he couldn't. He was her father. He had to be strong for her. So, he placed his hand on her until she sat up, hugging him until she fell asleep in his arms. He laid her down then slipped to his room. He took a long, hot shower, trying his best to wash the tension from his body and mind. But his mind wouldn't give in. He put on his pajamas then sat in front of the television, flipping channels before giving up then listening to Al Jarreau until he became drowsy. He decided to check on Gina before calling it a night.

He heard voices halfway down the hallway. At first, he thought Gina might be on the phone with one of her friends, but as he listened closely, he realized it wasn't her voice. It was a collection of voices, children and adults, male and female. He went to the window at the end of the hallway then peered outside; the streets were empty. Walking back to Gina's door he was sure the voices came from her room. He opened the door.

Gina sat on the floor beside the wall, a blank look on her face. Behind her the wall writhed with dozens of faces, their mouths spewing a torrent of words. Randolph lunged toward Gina, but something shoved him back.

"Betta listen!" the voices said in unison. *"Bring him back. Bring him back. Bring him back!"*

A bright light emerged from the wall surrounding Gina. She began to fade.

"No!" Randolph tried to reach her but he was pushed back again. He watched as she slowly faded then disappeared.

"Bring him back. You get her back. Betta listen!"

The last thing he saw of Gina was her eyes. Then the light and the faces were gone. He was alone in her room.

"Gina! Gina!" Randolph snatched open her closest. He looked under her bed. He ran through the house, searching every room as his voice went raw screaming her name. Randolph trudged back to her room then collapsed on the floor before the wall where she disappeared.

"Betta listen," the voices whispered. *"Bring the man back."*

"What man?" Randolph croaked.

"The man that lived here. The man that killed us."

He'd gone mad. The strain of Stephanie's death had driven him insane. Gina was somewhere in the house hiding from him, probably terrified of him.

"Gina, stop hiding and come on out," he said. "I'm okay."

"I'm not hiding, daddy," he heard her whisper. *"I'm with them."*

"It's going to be alright baby," he said. "Don't worry, it's going to be alright."

Randolph ran back to his room. He had no idea who owned this house before. He rummaged through his top dresser drawer until he found the

Sunshine Realty card. He punched the numbers on his phone with trembling fingers.

"This Ann Coolidge," the sweet southern voice said. "How can I help you?"

"Ann, this is Randolph, Randolph Chambers. You sold me the house in the Old Fourth Ward."

"Oh yes, Mr. Chambers! How is everything?"

"It's fine. Ann, I was wondering if you knew the person that owned this house previously."

There was silence for a moment. "Yes, I do. His name is Charles Wynn. He bought a house in Griffin. A small thing with a lot of land."

"He left a few things at the house. I'd like to ship them to him. Do you have the address?"

"Yes, I do. That's kind of you. Most people would just count it as a bonus. I'll text you the information tomorrow."

"I was wondering if you could send it tonight." Randolph struggled to keep his desperation out of his voice.

"Well, okay. Give me a minute. Nice talking to you Randolph."

"Same here, Ann."

Randolph hung up then immediately gazed at his screen. It took Ann thirty minutes to text the address. He immediately pulled up his GPS app then plugged in the address. As the GPS did its job, he went into his closet then opened the safe. Inside was a 9mm Glock, a clip, and a Taser. The Taser was Stephanie's; she refused to carry a gun. The voices said the mystery man was a murderer, so he wasn't taking any chances. He grabbed a coat and hat then hurried downstairs to the garage. There he found a new roll of duct tape. Not once did he hesitate, not once did he have second thoughts. He had to get Gina back.

By the time he got in the car the directions to Charles Wynn's house were plotted. He sped out of the neighborhood headed for Griffin. It was farther than he thought; when he reached the exit, he was low on gas. The GPS guided him down a dark lightless road bordered by pines and oaks, the shadowy wall of vegetation occasionally interrupted by farms or small homesteads.

"You have reached your destination," the GPS announced.

Randolph stopped his car before the open area. The grass rose high against the ragged barb wire fence, a damaged light flickering over the driveway entrance. The house stood about fifty yards from the road, so faking a broken-down car wouldn't work. He cut off his lights then drove up to the house, ignoring the no trespassing sign. There was no pretense to his actions; he had no time and no idea what he was doing.

He banged on the door. Hard footsteps advanced then stopped. The door jerked open.

Charles Wynn stood about Randolph's height but was powerfully built. A ragged beard covered his face. He glared at Randolph with bloodshot blue eyes.

"Who are you? What the hell are you doing here? What do you want?"

Randolph pulled out his gun with a shaky hand.

"I need you to come with me," he said.

Charles knocked the gun from his hand. It struck the porch then went off, shattering the nearby window. He grabbed Randolph's coat, jerked him inside then threw him across the room. Randolph crashed against the wall, blacking out for a moment.

"How did you find out?" Charles barked. "How?"

Randolph's sight cleared to Charles advancing on him with a knife. The blade was covered with blood. Randolph checked himself; it wasn't his. He looked about desperately then saw someone lying on the couch. It was a man, his eyes staring blankly into the ceiling. Blood ran down his shirt then dripped onto the brown carpet. Randolph pushed back his fear. He eased the taser out of his pocket then waited for the killer to come to him.

"Don't matter how you found out," he said. "Don't matter at all."

Randolph waited until Charles reached for him. He slapped the man's hand aside, drove the Taser into his chest then pressed the button. Charles shook, dropping the knife then collapsing to the floor. Randolph waited until he stopped convulsing then scrambled to his feet. He tased him again, ran outside for the duct tape then rushed back inside. Randolph fought to ignore the dead man on the couch, concentrating on his task. He taped Charles' feet together then taped his hands behind his back. He taped his mouth last. The man was heavy; he dragged him outside, waiting until he was near the car before lifting him up then dropping him into the trunk.

Then he sped away, driving back to the city. He waited until he was almost home before calling the Griffin police and reporting the dead man. He pulled into the garage then closed the door. When he opened the trunk Charles was conscious. There was no fear in his eyes, just anger as he struggled.

Randolph reached for him, but Charles rolled away, kicking at him with his bound legs. Randolph took out the taser; Charles pleaded with his eyes just before Randolph tased him. He waited a moment then lifted him from the trunk. Randolph struggled up the stairs, praying that none of the neighbors saw him carrying the man into the house. By the time he reached the inside stairs he was exhausted. He grabbed Charles's feet then dragged him up, the man's head bouncing off each step. He continued to drag him into Gina's room then collapsed on his ass exhausted. He glared at the wall.

"He's here!"

Faint mumbling danced about him.

"Where's my daughter?"

"He's here!" the voices shouted.

The faces appeared on the walls full of ecstatic smiles. The light that consumed Gina materialized over Charles. He came to as it descended on him, his screams muffled by the tape. The faces laughed in delight as their brightness enveloped the murderer, their glee increasing with each tortured scream. Then the light exploded, blinding Randolph. When his sight cleared Gina lay on the floor before him.

Randolph grabbed her, hugging her tight as tears streamed from his eyes.

"Daddy?" she said.

"Yes, baby, it's Daddy."

She hugged him back. "I saw momma."

Randolph pulled away from her. "What?"

"I saw momma. She told me to tell you that she loves and misses us. She told me to tell you not to worry. We'll be together again."

She looked in Gina's eyes. She was calm, her eyes peaceful.

Randolph hugged her again.

"Everything is going to be alright baby girl," he said. "It's going to be alright."

"I know daddy," Gina whispered. "You listened."

Johnson's Farm

They came for Cody Johnson on a moonless night after a summer downpour. Fog hid their approach through the pines, mist rising like steam from the grass, the air so humid it was hard to breath. Every man creeping across the wet ground had no remorse for what they were about to do. Niggers needed to know their place. They ought not reach for what they didn't deserve. The men felt justified in what they were about to do.

But Cody Johnson wasn't a fool. He slept with a double-barreled shotgun by his bed and a Colt revolver under his pillow. His hound dogs were trained to howl when the wind blew hard. He knew they would come for him eventually. And when they did, he'd be ready.

The dogs wailed and Johnson sat up in his bed. He grabbed his coveralls and shimmied into them. Cody took the Colt from under his pillow and put it in his right-hand pocket. Grabbing the shotgun, he ambled over to his bedroom window, the window that faced the woods behind the farm. The fog made it hard to see, but the dogs made it clear they were coming that way.

"I knows y'all out there!" Johnson shouted. "And I know why y'alls here. I'm giving y'all one chance to go on back home. One chance!"

The men kept coming. They thought there was no way Johnson would fire on them. He was signing his death sentence if he did.

Johnson went to his cabinet and got the shotgun shells. Shooting white me would get him lynched, but he was dead no matter what he did. But he wasn't leaving this world alone. He loaded the double-barrel and cocked back the hammers.

"One last chance!" he shouted.

Silas Cane, county deputy sheriff, and wizard of the local Ku Klux Klan had about enough of Johnson. He stood up straight, making himself seen.

"Shut up, nigger!" he shouted back. "You know good and damn well . . ."

Johnson fired both barrels into Silas's chest. The man flew back twenty feet then rolled until he stopped at the forest edge, dead as a doornail.

The other men pulled out guns and fired back as they fled for the woods, killing Cody's hounds. Johnson kept loading and shooting until he was out of shells. He took out the revolver and shot more, striking Billy Waynewright in the knee, crippling the butcher for life.

When Johnson finally ran out of bullets the Klan rushed in. Malcolm Coldwater was the first through the door. Johnson hit him square across the mouth with the shotgun butt. Malcolm fell to the ground cussing through his ruined teeth as the other men jumped over him and set about beating Johnson unconscious. Some of the men wanted to kill him right then and there, but Thom Crowder, president of Crowder County Banking and Savings wouldn't allow it. He was senior commander since Silas got blown to hell.

"We came to make an example out of this boy," he said. "And that's what we're going to do!"

They dragged Cody's unconscious body out of the house then loaded him into the back of Tim Foley's Ford pickup. The illicit caravan sped through the night to the massive red oak standing by the bank of Poor Man's Creek. They threw water on Johnson's face until he revived, tied a rope around his neck then strung it to a low thick branch on the tree.

"You asked for this, nigger!" Thom Crowder shouted. The men cheered his words. Johnson glared at them all, not one ounce of fear in his eyes.

"You sorry ass crackers come to take my land because you ain't good enough to build something for yourself. But I swear before God Almighty ain't nan one of y'all will ever live on my land. It's mine now, and it always will be!"

Johnson ended his words with a wad of spit that landed on Thom Crowder's shoe. Thom gave Tim the signal and Tim sped away. Johnson dropped, but the men didn't get the show they were expecting. Johnson hung rigid like a slab of meat in the smokehouse, glaring until the life left his eyes. Someone from the crowd doused his body with kerosene and lit it afire, the men watching Johnson burn until the rope snapped and the flaming body fell to the ground. The area was swept with a gust of wind that carried Johnson's ashes into the crowd, stinging the spectators' eyes and chilling them like a winter gale. The men hurried away; their nefarious deed done.

The sheriff waited three days before sending his deputies to investigate the 'disturbance' at the Johnson Farm. They walked around the house then returned to the station to file their bogus report. The Johnson farm was put up for sale, since Johnson was never married, had no children, and his kinfolks were too afraid to claim what belong to them. An auction was held two weeks after Johnson's disappearance. A few colored farmers tried to participate but were run off by the sheriff and his deputies. Thom Crowder placed the highest bid, and the Johnson farm became a part of his growing agricultural empire, added to his traditional family farm and the other land he'd acquired by foreclosure and paying delinquent taxes.

Thom paid a visit to the farm the next day. He was always impressed by Johnson's property. Cody did a good job keeping it productive, especially for a colored man. The fields were always neatly plowed and the harvests plentiful. His livestock was healthy and well groomed. The truth was Johnson's farm sat on some of the best farmland in the Georgia Heartland, blessed with timely rain and a natural spring that provided irrigation water during dry spells. Thom had big plans for the land; he was going to plant the largest peach grove the state had ever seen.

He was walking back to his car when he heard a strange sound coming from the well. Thom shuffled over with a frown. The last thing he needed was some animal carcass contaminating the well water. He took off his hat then peered inside, hoping to get a glimpse of the hapless beast. A chilling breeze swirled around his knees and Thom felt his feet lift from the ground. The last thing Thom Crowder saw on this earth was the sweet well water of Johnson's Farm.

Mr. Crowder's funeral was a spectacle. All the bank employees attended, as well as noted county officials and members of the Klan. The governor sent his representative; he didn't care much for Thom Crowder, seeing that the ambitious banker almost defeated him in the last election. No colored folks were in attendance, not that they would have been allowed if they tried. The county flags were flown at half-mast for a week in honor of a man who had spent his life in service to his fellow citizens and the State of Georgia.

The Johnson Farm was up for bid again. Crowder's only son, Bosephus, was not a farmer and had no aspirations of expanding the family holdings. His daughter Darlene had long abandoned the family for the cosmopolitan life in Atlanta, and her twin Sharlene was happy teaching third grade at the county elementary school for white children. A few colored farmers showed up again, and again they were turned away. Crowder was the richest man in the county, so the bidding didn't get as high. The farm was sold to the man who drove the truck from which Cody Johnson was hanged, Tim Foley.

The Foley clan had scratched a meager living from the Georgia red clay long before the state was a state. They were simple folk; their only significant achievements were losing eight male family members during the War of Northern Aggression and protecting their farm from roving Yankees during Sherman's march to the sea. The boys usually dropped out of school at eighth grade; the girls married and started families young. But Tim was bold. He fought against his daddy's wishes and graduated with a high school diploma and dreams of a better life. Those dreams were dashed when Tim's daddy died from a gunshot wound to the head during a disagreement after a game of dice behind Mr. Pritchard's country store. Since Tim was the eldest, the responsibility for the farm and the family fell on his narrow shoulders.

The added burden failed to extinguish Tim's backwoods dreams. He found his path to fortune making moonshine, using his home-grown skills to build the largest still in the county and providing the local honky-tonks with cheap spirits. The business wasn't as lucrative as he hoped; there were many hands he had to grease to keep the law looking the other way. When the Johnson Farm came up for bid again, Tim's goals were modest. He would clear the forest, selling the pines for pulpwood and the oaks for firewood. He'd divide the land into small plots and share-crop it to white and colored folks too poor to afford their own land.

Tim drove out to the land the day after he got the deed. The farm was still in good shape despite the lack of maintenance since Johnson's killing. He used the old key to enter the house; everything was in order, although a bit musty and dusty. He opened the windows to let in the fresh summer air. He had a mind to stay the night but thought better of it. His wife Daisy would think he was running around with Gertrude Potter. That was Wednesday night, but Daisy wouldn't care.

He strolled to the livestock pens near the woods. The chickens were nowhere to be found, but the mule was still in its gate, its ribs starting to show from lack of food. Tim couldn't have any animal dying on him, at least not until he carried out his plans. He located the barn and found a pile of hay. With the pitchfork he scooped up a mound and carried it to the mule, dropping it under the mule's head. The mule ate eagerly as Tim sauntered away, lighting a cigarette. As he walked behind the mule, a tooth chattering wind blew up on him. That same wind caught a mud dauber, pushing the insect into the mule's flanks. The mud dauber stung the mule; the mule cried out in pain then kicked, its rear hooves colliding with Tim's head and sending him into the Great Beyond.

Daisy found Tim's body three days later. She came to the farm with a pistol in her hand after going to Gertude's house and giving her an ass whupping she'd never forget. Daisy called the sheriff; the deputies arrived an hour later and declared Tim's death accidental. Tim's relatives built him a fine casket and buried him in the family cemetery beside daddy and the family war heroes. Once again, his ambitions had been denied. The Johnson Farm was up for bid once more. The Foley family was too poor to maintain it, especially with Tim's untimely demise. The colored folks didn't show this time. They knew better. Johnson's Farm was meant to stay his, and although he failed to protect it in the here and now, he was doing a fine job from the hereafter.

A crowd formed on the county courthouse steps, much smaller than previously and with much less enthusiasm. The man who won the bid wasn't a county resident; hc hailcd from nearby Tidwell County and was unknown to everyone in attendance. He paid for the land in cash right after the auction was complete, took the deed, hurried to his car then sped away. His name was Billy Ray Calhoun.

Billy Ray Calhoun was a respectable man, as good as a white man could be for the times. Although he was a staunch believer in white supremacy, he also believed that the Negro race should be respected and allowed to accomplish whatever its limited skills could achieve. He was well aware of the strange occurrences of Johnson's Farm, but unlike others, Billy had connections in the Negro community. Not only did he know what plagued the farm, he also knew the solution.

Billy hired Tommy Small to take him into nearby Cooter Swamp where Miss Hattie resided. Tommy made him pay double the price just in case Miss Hattie cursed them both and he had to buy root remedies. It took half the day to reach the pine rise where Miss Hattie lived, a tiny island surrounded by tea-colored water and cypress trees draped with Spanish moss. Billy stepped gingerly onto the moss-covered ground and tipped toward the house. It was a beacon of beauty surrounded by the dismal, a well-made structure painted white with blue windows and a blue door to keep the haints out. A small broom leaned against an old rocking chair, another precaution for any witches that might try to enter. Billy knocked on the door.

"Is that you Billy Calhoun?" a high-pitched voice called out.

Billy hesitated before answering. He had not informed Miss Hattie of his visit.

"Ye . . . Yes, Miss Hattie! It's Billy Calhoun."

"Come on in here!"

Billy entered the house and was greeted by the smell of moth balls and jasmine. Miss Hattie's parlor was well arranged; there was no better furnished room south of Macon.

"Take a seat," Miss Hattie called out. "I'll be in directly."

Billy sat in the plush chair near the door just in case he had to make a hasty exit. Miss Hattie entered the room moments later, and Bill Calhoun was stunned. The rumors said that Miss Hattie was as old as the swamp and twice as ugly. The truth was the exact opposite. Miss Hattie stood as tall as most men, with smooth black skin and a pleasant youthful face that contrasted with silver

gray hair piled atop her head. She wore a flowered house dress that hugged her shapely body
near her breasts and hips. Miss Hattie carried a
tray with two cups of steaming liquid.

"Hello, Billy," she said in a pleasant disarm-
ing tone. "Do you like what you see?"

Billy turned red as a beet. "I must say I do,
Miss Hattie."

Miss Hattie chuckled. "I meant the furniture.
Had it shipped all the way from New Orleans."

"Of course," Billy replied. "It's beautiful."

Miss Hattie offered Billy tea, then sat on the
sofa on the opposite side of the room. Billy
sipped his tea and felt a calm pass through his
body. Miss Hattie grinned as if she knew what he
experienced.

"This is excellent tea," he said.

"I know," Miss Hattie replied. "It was Cody's
favorite. He loved it as much as he loved his
farm."

A chill gripped Billy as Miss Hattie uttered
those words. He placed down his cup.

"That's what I'm here to discuss, Miss
Hattie," he said. "You probably already know
that I purchased the deed to Cody's farm."

"Mr. Johnson to you," Miss Hattie said. "We's
related on my mama's side. You didn't know the
man, and you don't have the right to call him by
his first name."

"I apologize," Billy said. "I never meant to of-
fend. People in my county know that I have always thought well of the Negro race."

"Let's get down to it," Miss Hattie said. "You want me to help you lay claim to Cody's farm. You want me to lay Cody's spirit to rest."

"Yes, I do," Billy replied. "And I'm willing to pay whatever it takes to do so."

"Five thousand dollars," Miss Hattie said.

Billy almost fell out of his chair. "What?!?"

"You heard me right," Miss Hattie replied. "Cody never was able to get his full due from his land because of white folks, and I know full well what that land will be worth in your hands. You'll make more than enough."

Billy rubbed his chin. "Still, that's a lot of money . . ."

"For a nigger?" Miss Hattie finished. "You have a choice, Billy. Pay me and claim Cody's farm or leave."

"Mama?"

Billy looked to the source of the voice. A girl stood in the kitchen doorway, the mirror image to Miss Hattie. Miss Hattie looked at the girl and frowned.

"Go on now girl," she said. "This is grown folks' business."

"Yes ma'am," the girl said. She glanced at Billy then backed into the darkness. Billy heard a screen door creak open then slam.

"A sweet looking child," Billy commented. "Who's her daddy?"

"That's none of your business," Miss Hattie said. "Do we have a deal?"

Billy leaned back into his chair. "Five thousand dollars is a lot of money for anyone. But I understand what you're doing. You're looking out for yourself and your child. I think twenty-five hundred is good enough."

Miss Hattie stood. "It was nice meeting you, Billy. I wish you luck with your new farm."

Billy jumped to his feet.

"That's it? You're not open to haggling?"

"No," Miss Hattie replied. "Five thousand or nothing."

Billy surrendered. "I don't have that kind of money right now."

"When you get it, send it by Tommy," Miss Hattie said. "I'll send you what you need."

"How do I know I can trust you," Billy asked.

"You don't," Miss Hattie replied. "It's a risk you'll have to take. Goodbye, Billy. See yourself out."

Billy Calhoun left Miss Hattie's house in a quandary. He'd purchased the Johnson Farm for much less that it was worth, yet Miss Hattie's deal would bring the price slightly higher than he'd planned. But he had no choice. Cody Johnson's spirit had to be quelled.

Three days after their meeting Billy Calhoun returned to Miss Hattie's house with five thousand dollars. He knocked on the door. Instead of Miss Hattie, the girl greeted him. She held a burlap sack in one hand and a small box in the other.

"Mama told me to give you this," she said.

Billy took the bag and the box. He placed them on the porch then handed the girl an envelope with the money.

"You make sure your Mama gets that, okay?" he said.

The girl frowned. "I ain't no thief."

"I know," Billy said. "Tell your mama I said thank you."

Billy picked up the items and began to leave.

"What a minute," the girl said.

She handed Billy a folded piece of paper.

"Instructions," she said.

"Thank . . ."

The girl closed the door on him. Billy unfolded the note and read it on his way back.

Inside the bag is another bag. After the next rain, spread the contents on the grounds as well as you can. Once that's done, build a small fire outside the barn. Take half the contents of the small box and throw it into the fire. Take the rest of it home and brew it. Sprinkle a little on your shoes, then drink the rest. Cody won't worry you no more.

Miss Hattie

Billy did as Miss Hattie instructed. The rain that soaked the farm appeared like divine intervention, a brief summer squall that released its blessing only on the farm and the nearby woods. Billy arrived on the property a few hours later, spreading the odoriferous concoction over the grounds. It took a moment to start a fire on the damp grass; once it was lit Billy tossed half the contents of the box into the flames and was rewarded with the pleasant aroma of Miss Hattie's excellent tea. The fragrance cancelled out the contents of the bag, restoring order to the farm. Billy drove home, kissing his wife and patting his dog's head before brewing the tea. He dribbled the tea on his shoes as instructed, then spent the evening enjoying the remaining brew while reading the newspaper. Billy slept peacefully, expectant of the days ahead.

The next morning Billy's wife, Cindy, awoke and prepared breakfast. She called out for her husband, then went to find him when he didn't answer. Billy lay in the bed with a pleasant look on his face. His wife grinned, then shook her husband to wake him. His head fell at an odd angle, and his wife covered her mouth in shock. Billy Calhoun had died in his sleep with dreams of the Johnson Farm.

The county coroner announced his findings on Billy's death two weeks after it occurred. Billy had been poisoned. The initial suspicion went to his wife, but everyone who knew the Calhouns vouched for Cindy and her fathomless love for her husband. Word spread that Billy was seen going into the swamp a few days before his death. Time passed and whispers became rumors. Those rumors were enough for the Klan. On a moonless night they gathered at the edge of Cooter Swamp, piled into their johnboats, and set off for Miss Hattie's home. Once they reached isolated abode, they opened fire, tearing the house apart with buck shot and 30/30 rounds. They landed their boats in an invasion of white robes, bursting into the house to see their handiwork firsthand. They were disappointed. There was no one inside; nobody to claim and defile. They looted the home of whatever furniture or items undamaged by their gunfire then set the house ablaze.

Johnson's Farm was up for bid. This time, no one came. The message was clear to both Negroes and White folks; Johnson's farm belonged to Cody Johnson. Since none of Cody's relatives came forward to claim it, the land became county property, where it languished, nature claiming what once belonged to her. Buildings decayed and collapsed. The only structure that withstood time was Johnson's house. Though vines found purchase on the walls, the building refused to succumb. It was as if Cody Johnson was inside holding up the walls himself.

Decades came and went. The world changed and the state reluctantly conformed. The latest governor announced a highway would be built running the length of the state, and that highway would run through the county. Of course, those privy to such information quickly purchased the land the state would claim, all except Johnson's Farm. The highway came through with an army of bulldozers, levelers, and pavers, bringing a level of prosperity the county had never seen. Tax revenues swelled, as did the pockets of the county officials. But due to the attention of the state and the country, the old political system was dismantled. The new 'liberal' residents of the county clashed with the down-home folks as the county was dragged kicking and screaming into the 21st century. Through all the change and turmoil, Johnson's Farm was untouched.

* * *

One warm day in March, ten minutes after the property office of the new county government building opened for business, the old-time bell rang as a tall umber skinned woman entered the building walking with a regal stride. Her floral print dress matched the headwrap that hugged her perfect afro, her matching hoop earrings and septum ring complementing her bracelets. The clerk looked at her in wonder; she was definitely not from around these parts.

"May I help you?" the clerk asked with a syrupy southern drawl.

"Yes," the woman answered. "I'd like to inquire about the purchase a certain property."

"Do you have any paperwork?" the clerk asked.

"Yes."

The woman handed the clerk the survey papers. "I think it's called Johnson's Farm."

The clerk tensed. She unrolled the survey documents then nodded.

"Yes, this is the property," she said.

"Excellent!" The woman took off her shades, revealing her dark brown eyes. "Do you know who I should speak to about purchasing the land?"

"The land belongs to the county," the woman said. "Although I'm not sure you would want to purchase it."

The woman's smile faded. "Is it for sale?"

"Yes."

"Then I wish to purchase it."

The clerk hesitated and the woman rolled her eyes.

"This isn't about to get racial, is it?" she said. "Because if it is, I'm more than willing . . ."

The clerk shook her head. "No, no. It's not that. Claymont County is very progressive. It's just . . ."

"Just what?"

The clerk hesitated. She wasn't about to get tangled in a racial discrimination lawsuit over a haunted piece of property. Besides, whoever this woman was, she wasn't local. She wasn't worth the warning.

"Nothing, ma'am," the clerk said. "I apologize if I offended you."

"Apology accepted," the woman said with a smile. "My lawyer will be here in a week to oversee the details. I hope the land will still be available."

"It will," the clerk said.

"Thank you so much," the woman replied. She turned with a flourish and strode out of the building, leaving a vacuum of style in her wake.

Her lawyer arrived a week later as she promised, and after eighty years Johnson's Farm had a new owner. The legal documents listed the woman's name as Naomi Sunshine. As was the nature of folks in Claymont County, the local folks tried to discover who was this woman and why she'd come to the county. Some said she favored the Dawsons; others thought she might be related to that Rooks boy who played quarterback for Fox Valley State College then went to the pros. Whoever she was, Naomi came to Claymont County with a purpose. Not only did she buy Johnson's property, but she also purchased the old Crowder land and the pine plantation that used to be Foley property. But the only property she developed was Johnson's Farm. Every company hired to do the work on the property was Black owned. If a local Black company wasn't available, a company was hired from out of town. The property was cleared, and a small home was constructed a few yards behind the original home. It was when renovations began on the original home that the locals took notice. Although most of the people who lived during those earlier dark days had gone on to Glory, the story of Johnson Farm lingered. Would some tragedy befall Miss Sunshine? Only time would tell.

Miss Sunshine's plans for the old house were revealed when she finally applied for a business permit. The house was to be transformed into a vegan restaurant, the first in the county. Most of the vegetables would be grown on the farm. Miss Sunshine hired local Black farmers to clear, plant, and maintain the land. By the time Miss Sunshine returned she'd become a local celebrity. The restaurant opened with great fanfare and became an instant success. Sunshine, as the restaurant was named, became a favorite stop for the health-conscious road weary and the local vegan community. Naomi was the perfect hostess;

although she didn't work in the restaurant, she would often stroll from her house to talk to customers or would be seen tending the fields or her garden. Local and state news channels clamored to interview this young, budding entrepreneur but she refused them all.

Fulton Albright, station owner of WTAQ TV, The Sound of the South, arrived at his office Monday morning and received a pleasant surprise. The mysterious Naomi Sunshine finally agreed to an interview! She requested Brandon Calhoun, which was a great choice. Fulton assembled his crack team and sent them immediately to the restaurant. Naomi greeted them with her warm smile, leading the crew to a table near the busy kitchen. Brandon Calhoun, a straw blonde local boy, former football standout and Communications graduate from University of Georgia, flashed his perfect smile as he entered the establishment. When they reached the table, Brandon, being the southern gentleman that he was, pulled Naomi's chair out for her before sitting and checking his mike.

"Thank you for allowing us to interview you, Miss Sunshine," he said.

"It's my pleasure," Naomi replied.

"I must say you've accomplished so much in a short period of time."

"It's my nature," Naomi replied. "Once I set my mind on something, it gets done with a quickness."

Brandon laughed. "You've put Claymont County on the map. You could have built your restaurant anywhere. Why here?"

"I wanted to return to my roots," Naomi said.

Brandon's eyebrows rose. "Your roots?"

"Yes. I grew up in Atlanta, but my great grandmother was from Claymont."

"This is fascinating!" Brandon said. "My family had been here for generations. She may be someone I know."

"That's likely," Naomi replied. "My grandmother told me there were a few good white people in the county back in the day. Maybe your family was in that group."

"I would like to think so," Brandon said. "Thank goodness for progress."

"Indeed," Naomi replied.

A waiter came from the kitchen carrying a tray with two cups and a teapot.

"Ah," Brandon said. "Is this some of Miss Sunshine's famous organic tea?"

"Yes, it is," Naomi said.

"I've been dying to try it."

Naomi poured Brandon a cup and he took a sip.

"This is fantastic," he said.

"Thank you. It's a blend handed down from my great grandmother. The rumor is that she was a root worker."

Brandon sipped more tea before placing his cup down. "Let's talk about that," Brandon said.

"Well, the family story is that my great grandmother came into some money then left the county and moved to Atlanta. She started a business selling home remedies. She was able to send my grandmother to college. She graduated from Spelman then moved to Washington D.C. My mother and I were born there."

"And your mother?"

"She graduated from Howard and became a doctor."

Brandon sipped more tea. "I guess the medical profession wasn't for you?"

"It wasn't my cup of tea," Naomi replied with smile.

"And the rest is history," Brandon said. "You know I have a link to this property as well. My great grandfather owned it briefly. Unfortunately, he took ill and died before he could develop it."

"You mean Bill Calhoun?"

Brandon's smile faded.

"Yes. That's him."

Naomi smiled. "I did my research, too. My great grandmother was known around here as Miss Hattie. Miss Hattie Johnson, to be exact. My grandmother was five when they left the county."

Brandon winced and rubbed his stomach.

"It seems this tea doesn't agree with me."

"Really? I'm surprised."

Brandon stood and wobbled.

"I think we're done here," he said. "It was interesting talking to you, Naomi."

"Miss Sunshine," Naomi corrected. "Before you go. I have something for you."

Brandon's eyebrows rose. "For me?"

"Well, not exactly."

Naomi reached behind the counter and picked up a pink envelope.

"Give this to your grandmother. She's still with us, isn't she?"

"Yes, she is. She lives in Tidwell County."

Naomi smiled. "That's nice. You make sure she gets that."

Brandon nodded. "I will."

The TV crew packed up their gear and left the restaurant, headed back to the station with the scoop of the year. Later that day Brandon drove out to Grandma Betty's house. Grandma Betty sat on the screened in front porch as she always did in the afternoon, enjoying the sun and her azaleas. Brandon sauntered up to the porch, the pink envelope from Miss Sunshine in his hand. She greeted her grandson with a hug and kiss.

"Grandma, I interviewed Naomi Sunshine today," Brandon said.

"That colored girl who owns the restaurant off the highway?" Grandma said.

Brandon frowned. "We don't call them colored anymore. Anyway, she told me to give you this."

Brandon handed his grandma the envelope. Betty opened it.

"I can't read this," she said. "Go get me my glasses."

Brandon entered the house and found grandma's reading glasses on the coffee table in the parlor. He carried them back to her. Betty put on her glasses and read the paper. It was a check written to her daddy, Billy Calhoun, for five thousand dollars. Included with the check was a note. Grandma read it.

"Oh . . ." she fainted.

Brandon shook his grandma back to consciousness.

"What's wrong?" he asked.

Grandma gave him the note.

"Hope you enjoyed the tea."
Miss Hattie

* * *

Naomi Sunshine sat on her front porch, rocking back and forth in her swing chair. She gazed upon the land she owned, proud that she was able to claim what was rightfully hers. A warm breeze flowed over her and she smiled.

"Thank you, Uncle Cody," she whispered. "Thank you for holding on."

MILTON J DAVIS

Bloodline

(Previously published in Slay: Stories of the Vampire Noire)

-1-

We were cruising down Peachtree Street when
Kerry got pissed. It was midnight; despite his
treatments he still preferred to go out after sundown, especially on cloudy nights. The streets
were slick from the recent summer shower, so I
told him to slow down.

"What? You afraid we might have an accident?" He smiled at me devilishly.

"That's easy for you to laugh at," I replied.
"I'm new."

Kerry jerked the steering wheel and we drifted
left off Peachtree to International. We plunged
down the steep hill before he slammed on the
brakes at the intersection. An Inquisitor standing
on the corner by Peachtree Plaza glared at us
from behind his facemask, his lance aimed in our
direction. Kerry gripped the steering wheel
tighter, the veins in his hands and forearms visible.

"Kerry, don't," I whispered.

"Fucking overseers," he whispered back.

Kerry was angry, but he wasn't a fool. That
lance would spit a streak of angel fire that would
smoke both of us in seconds. He waited for the
light to turn green then pulled away slowly. We
stopped again at the light before Centennial Park
then turned left again, migrating around the park

to the light between Phillips Arena and the CNN center.

"I'm hungry," I said.

Kerry looked at me with a frown. "You expect me to take you all the way back home so you can eat?"

"No, there's an open market nearby," I answered.

"Where?"

"In Midtown near Ponce City Market."

The light turned green and Kerry slammed on the gas, leaving a blue-white cloud of smoke. I felt sorry for him. I was born after the Inquisition, so life had always been this way for me. Kerry was old school, a Trueblood. He looked my age, but he was at least seven hundred years old. He'd known only one way to live and that had been stripped from him by the Church. Once the scientists identified the genetic codes that revealed what we were, it was easy for the Inquisitors to hunt us down and kill us. We were rounded up and locked in internment camps until the See could determine what to do with us. The others weren't so lucky. We had always been popular in a morbid sort of way so there were Believers that spoke for our salvation. The others were killed where they stood; werewolves, witches, and warlocks slaughtered by the Inquisitors and their angel fire staffs. At least that's what I was taught in history class. The same scientists that discovered how to identify and kill us produced a way to fix us. It involved a series of treatments that would convert our DNA and make us almost normal. But some things they couldn't change.

Kerry drove to the market without my directions. He pretended earlier not to know but I knew he did. All of us do.

"Hurry up," he said.

I got out of the car and entered Sunshine Market. I was dressed for date night; my skirt was short and my blouse low cut. My hair floated over my head in an afro; this time of year was too humid so I just let it go natural. The men in the market leered at me until it became clear where I was headed. Their looks became frowns of disgust. By the time I reached the back of the market the only person paying attention to me was Jackie Zhang.

"Whoa, Telisa! You look good tonight!"

"Watch it, Jackie," I warned. "Mrs. Zhang might hear you. You got some fruit?"

Jackie grinned. "Just got some in today. Good ones, too" He reached under the counter and brought up a large blood fruit. The veins pulsed close to the surface and my stomach growled.

"Do all of them look like this one?"

"Yep."

"I'll take four."

Jackie bagged them up. "This is a lot of fruit for one person."

"I'm with Kerry."

Jackie frowned. "I don't see why you spend time with that low life."

It was my turn to frown. "Shut it, Jackie. You're not my daddy. How much?"

"It's on the house tonight."

"You're so sweet!" I leaned over the counter and kissed him on the cheek. "Tell Mrs. Zhang I said hi."

Kerry was still mean mugging when I got back to the car.

"What took you so long?"

I jumped in the car and took a blood fruit from the bag. "Me and Jackie were talking."

"That dirty old bastard makes me sick."

"Everybody makes you sick." I bit into the blood fruit, my fangs sinking into a thick vein. It was a juicy one; the warm red fluid ran down my cheek.

"Want one?" I offered.

Kerry looked away. "I'm not hungry."

I shrugged and enjoyed my meal. The boys in the white coats failed to curb our cravings completely, so they developed blood fruit. It's not really fruit, but a simple organism that produces human blood. They're great, but the old heads think they're disgusting. They prefer the alternative, but the alternative will get you smoked.

We were rolling through Buckhead when things got funky. We stopped at a red light at the corner of Peachtree and Pharr. A swarm of party goers crossed before us, young men and women smelling and looking good.

"That's what we should be enjoying," Kerry said.

"Stop it, Kerry," I replied.

"They used to fear us, now they just laugh at us."

"The light's green," I said.

Kerry ignored me; his eyes locked on the young throng forming a line into the nightclub. Then he slammed on the gas and we sped toward downtown.

"Slow down, Kerry," I said.

He kept speeding until we were downtown. He swung into a parking lot and grabbed my wrist, pulling me out of the car. I had to run to keep up with him, he was walking so fast.

"What's going on?" I said. I was excited and nervous.

He led me into a narrow alley, spun me about and kissed me. I kissed him back hard, moaning as his hand moved down my back and under my skirt. This wasn't the first time we'd done it in public, but something about this time was different. I was working my hands down his pants when he pushed me away.

"Wait here," he said.

"What?"

"Wait here. I'll be right back."

I was stunned. One minute my man was feeling me up in an alley and the next minute he was gone. Before I could get angry, he was back.

"I brought you something," he said.

It was a man. He was dressed in a concierge uniform, his eyes half closed.

"Now here's a real meal!" He jerked the man up and bit his neck. The man moaned but didn't struggle as Kerry drank his blood. He dropped the man then came to me. I backed away.

"Kerry, I don't want any part of this," I said. He gripped the back of my head and kissed me. I tasted blood on his lips, blood like I never tasted before. It was so warm and so…sweet. I ran my tongue through his mouth, savoring the trickle of blood still there.

Kerry pulled away. "See? This is what we were meant to have."

A bright light flooded the alley, blinding us.

"They're in here!" a voice shouted. "Send back up!"

An inquisitor emerged from the light, his lance tip glowing. Kerry shoved me aside and leaped higher than I'd ever seen anyone leap. Angel fire burned over my head as I fell. My head struck the ground and I was stunned for a minute; when my vision cleared Kerry and the Inquisitor were struggling in front of me. The lance was broken. The two of them were slamming each other against the walls. I heard a lot of footsteps heading towards the alley.

Kerry lifted the Inquisitor off the ground by the neck with both hands. He pinned him against the wall and looked at me.

"Get out of here!" he shouted.

"Kerry, no!" I pleaded. "Let him go. They're going to kill you."

"Living like this, I'm already dead." He smiled at me. "Remember what you are. Remember what it's like."

A squad of Inquisitors charged into the alley. Kerry threw his Inquisitor at them then leaped into their midst. I ran in the other direction, escaping into the parking lot. The concierge was there propped against the wall, trying to stop the bleeding from his neck. I rushed him, knocking his hand away and digging my fangs into his neck. The taste was exhilarating. He tried to struggle but I held him still, surprised at my strength. I drank until there was nothing left, the concierge limp in my arms. Angel fire flashed from the alley; I dropped the body and ran.

I don't know whether to thank Kerry or curse him. He's dead so I can't do either. The Inquisitors are hunting me, calling me a backslider. If I turned myself in and confessed, I would be rehabilitated. But I can't. It's just too good. I feel better and stronger that I ever have. Kerry told me to remember what I am, but the reality is I never knew. Now I do. I can never go back.

-2-

I love the feeling of night. I love the way the shadows caress my shoulders and obscure my flaws. I revel in coolness that exists in the dark despite the time of year. Most of all, I love how the night brings out the best and the worst in us all, the absence of sunlight a shield that hides our actions, whatever they might be.

I understand now why the old ones hunted at night. The light was their enemy, revealing the natural urge in them considered vile and grotesque by the others. Kerry was an old one, preferring the darkness despite the freedom of the Inquisition. I never understood, until now.

I had been a backslider for two years, seven hundred and thirty days of hunting and being hunted. I smelled, my clothes were ragged and my hair had twisted into knots. Sometimes I tried to hate Kerry for introducing me to this life, but most of the time I rarely thought of him. I was consumed with the hunger and the pursuit of prey. There was no other feeling.

The Inquisitors made themselves known by their attempt at stealth. The abandoned building I called home teemed with the homeless, their coming and going a parade of curses, clanging and crunching. The fact that the Inquisitors tried to be silent gave them away. I crouched in filth, closing my eyes to see with my other senses. It was one of the changes that occurred after I began feeding the old way. My entire being transformed, tuned to my prey's existence like a lion instinctively knows the ways of the antelope. The men reeked; their pheromones making them easy to spot. Someone else lurked among them, a person whose image was less distinct. It was a woman. Her scent was an irritant to me; it seems I was meant to hunt men. Her presence caused a problem, especially if she broke away from the others. She did.

I worked my way towards the rear of the building, expecting to escape out of the back door leading into a trash strewn alley and into the streets. I was about to turn when I felt cold metal press against my back and a sharp prick in my neck.

"Come with me," the woman ordered. I expected her to lead me towards her companions. Instead she took me where I was headed, the alleyway.

"Turn around," she said. I turned and looked into her stern face. She was pretty, strands of black hair escaping from beneath her helmet. "Remember my face. I'll meet you here tomorrow."

"Why should I come back if you're letting me go?"

"You have a nano GPS swimming in your veins. If you try to leave town within the next forty-eight hours, I'll call a team, tell them where you are and you'll get smoked."

"I could just turn myself in for redemption."

She smiled. "Not you. Besides, I can get you out of here."

"Where?" I asked.

"Somewhere safe," she answered. "Somewhere vampires aren't hated or hunted."

I was angry and confused. "Why are you doing this?"

Her face changed, a shadow of sorrow flashing across her eyes. "I need your help."

I heard chatter spilling from her earpiece and her face became stern again. "Remember. Here. Tomorrow. Now go."

She stepped aside and I ran into the alley. The darkness proved no problem for me because the other side effect of my new feeding habits was excellent night vision. I had morphed into a predator, my physical senses enhanced and attuned to my prey. It was a waste. I wasn't hunting down wary Homo sapiens in dense forests; I was swatting them like flies in a human trash heap. All I had to do was reach out and dinner was served. My only obstacle was the Inquisitors and they were easy to avoid.

Leaving the slums meant changing my appearance. I jumped alleyways and vacant lots until I reached Buckhead then did a quick smash and grab on an upscale jeans boutique. I washed up the best I could at the Marta station and changed. With the exception of makeup, I cleaned up pretty good. Old memories crept into my head; the days when men looked at me with desire until they saw my fangs. Now they didn't bother. I was just another homeless bitch to be used or avoided, except when they approached me to have a little fun, they found the tables turned.

I was hungry beyond belief when I returned to the building the next day. The woman was waiting. She looked different out of uniform, cute, actually. Her long hair was pulled back into a ponytail that teased the small of her back. She wore a white blouse and short blue jean mini skirt, showing off her toned legs. It was a dangerous way to dress in that part of town, but she was an Inquisitor. She could handle herself. She spotted me and waved me over. She was inside her Jeep as I walked up. The passenger door swung open, almost hitting me.

"Get in," she ordered.

I hesitated then sat. A grocery bag rested on the floor between us; I knew what it was before she said a word.

"Eat, but not too much. I need you hungry."

I reached into the bag and pulled out a pulsing blood fruit. It had been so long since I fed on the placebo that I had no appetite for it. I bit into it anyway and was pleasantly surprised. It was better than I remembered. Not good, but good enough.

The woman sped off, working her way out of the slums and onto 75/85. We headed north out of the city and into the mountains. We were both quiet, her eyes locked on the road, my eyes locked on her. I was reaching for another blood fruit and she grabbed my wrist.

"That's enough," she barked.

I've never bitten anyone out of anger, but I was coming damn close.

"What's your name?" I asked.

"It doesn't matter," she replied. "It's best you don't know. Better for both of us."

Our journey ended on a dirt road before a redwood cabin. The woman jumped out the Jeep and ran to the door. I followed as I was expected to. The inside of the cabin was modest, similar to a studio apartment. There was a small kitchen, an old couch and a DTV hanging on the wall. A double bed sat in the corner of the cabin, occupied by a man hooked to an IV. The woman grabbed my arm and towed me to the bedridden man.

"What wrong with him?" I asked.

"Cancer," she said, her voice trembling. "Terminal."

"So why am I here?"

She looked at me and I couldn't tell if she was angry or desperate.

"Bite him."

I was stunned. I looked at her and read the certainty in her eyes.

"So, you want me to kill him, to put him out of his misery?"

She laughed. "I want you to do just the opposite. I want you to heal him."

"Look, if I bite him, I kill him."

She laughed again, which pissed me off. "You should look behind you once you're done eating. Every person you've bitten has lived. Better still, they come back just like you."

"Bullshit," was all I could say.

"That's why the Church wants you dead. You're a vampire virus. It wasn't supposed to be like this."

She sat in a metal folding chair by the man's head and whispered to him in Spanish.

"You were created to scare people back to the church. You, werewolves, witches, all of you. Once the Redemption began, they eliminated all the freaks except vampires. They saw possibilities in you, clues to immortality. You're the first one to prove that it's possible."

I wanted to sit. No, I wanted to faint, but I was too mad.

"So, they want me so they can dissect me and study me."

The woman nodded. I looked at her man, his skin grayish, his chest barely rising and falling.

"If I bite him, he'll be like me."

The woman looked at me with pleading eyes.

"I know, but he'll be alive."

So I bit him. I could taste the cancer in him but I drank. I quickly remembered why I gave up blood fruit. I took my fill then stopped, wiping my mouth with my sleeve.

"Now what?"

The woman stroked the man's hair for a moment then went to the tiny chest at the foot of the bed.

"Sit down," she ordered.

I sat on the edge of the bed.

"This is going to hurt," she said.

I felt a sharp pain at the base of my neck. After a few uncomfortable minutes, the pain subsided.

"What was that?" I asked.

"I deactivated the tracker," the woman replied. "Stand up."

I stood. The woman opened the chest where I sat, took out a satchel, and gave it to me.

"These documents will get you into Canada. From there you can go to Europe. I've heard they don't hunt your kind there. A few people actually worship you."

For the last two years I existed in a daze, thinking of nothing but feeding. It never occurred to me that I was being hunted beyond redemption. I never considered leaving Atlanta, let alone the country. But if what the woman said was true, I was marked for death.

I took the tickets. The woman tossed me the keys to the Jeep.

"Take it," she said. "I won't need it for a while."

I looked at her and the man. He was breathing deeper and the color had come back to his skin.

"He'll get hungry eventually," I said.

She looked hopeful. "I know."

"Give him the fruit," I advised. "Never let him bite a person, not even you."

She looked at me and smiled. "Thank you."

I turned away and headed for the door.

"My name is Maria," she called out.

"Goodbye, Maria," I said.

"Goodbye, Telisa," she replied. "God bless you."

I hesitated and then stepped out the door into the night.

-3-

Sometimes enough is enough. It's like you look around and realize you made a very bad mistake. At that point you know you have two choices. You can go back to where you started, or you can continue forward and hope for the best. But one thing you can't do. You can't sit still because if you stop, you'll die. It's that simple. Or at least it should be.

I'd never driven through snow. I spent my entire life in the South and the only snow I ever saw occurred before I could drive. So, I was surprised at how well I handled the heavy snowfall as I travelled through Michigan. I was on my way to Detroit. If all went well, I'd cross into Windsor, Canada, and after a few more days I'd be on my way to Europe. Maria supplied me with the documents I needed to get into Canada, and I'd done the best I could to change my appearance. The DIY perm job was bad, yet good enough. I sobbed when I compressed my afro, but pride had to give way to survival.

For days I'd been living out of my car, afraid to check into a hotel and be discovered. My name and face were everywhere, as well it should be. The blood fruit didn't satisfy me any longer. I had to have human blood. Sometimes I managed to break into a blood bank and steal bags of plasma, but they were only a little more filling than blood fruit, the artificial blood pod designed to keep me and those like me in check. Kerry said he was liberating me that day; he said he was showing me what I truly was. I curse the day I met him.

The hotel I booked was on the outskirts of the city. I was sure of my disguise, but I wasn't taking any chances. I was only a few miles from freedom and I wasn't going to fuck it up. The check-in clerk, an older woman with pasty skin and thinning hair, barely paid attention to me as I gave her my false information and paid for my room cash. But I paid attention to her. I could feel her blood pulsing through her veins. A sharp pang in my gut caused me to wince.

"You alright, honey?" she asked.

I looked into her ruddy eyes and felt her concern.

"I'm okay," I replied. "Just a little hungry."

"There's a diner a mile down the road," the woman replied. "It's open twenty-four hours. The lunch and dinner menu sucks, but their breakfast is to die for."

I stared at the woman a moment longer then forced a smile to my face.

"I'll be okay. I'm going into the city."

The woman shrugged then handed me my key card. "Have a nice stay. If there's anything wrong with your room, give me a call."

I took the key card then hurried to my room. By the time I reached it, my hands trembled so badly I could barely insert the card into the slot. I finally unlocked the door then stormed in. I flung my backpack onto the room, closed and locked the door then hurried back to my car. I needed to feed.

It seemed like hours before I reached the city. I didn't know anything about Detroit, but I've been hunting long enough to find what I was craving for. I made a left turn off the main thoroughfare and found myself in the club district. A long line snaked from a non-descript building with a glaring neon sign. The name made no difference to me; I focused on the club goers waiting to enter. I parked in the nearest parking lot then walked fast toward the club. I didn't have to complete my journey; a man entered the parking lot, whistling as he strolled to his car. I hurried

toward him, a smile on my face. He smiled back;
apparently, he thought I was attractive.

"What's up, baby girl?" he said.

I pushed him against the nearest car then sank
my teeth deep into his throat. He struggled, but I
was stronger, much stronger. I drained him then
dropped his body like an empty shell. But I was
still hungry. A woman entered the parking lot,
her eyes darting about like women do when
walking into a parking lot alone. She saw me and
relaxed; I almost felt sorry for her. I pounced on
her as she opened her car door. I pushed her inside to the passenger side then bit into her neck.
Her screams subsided quickly as I drank. I left
her limp in the seat.

I hurried back to my car, the bottom half of
my face and the front of my shirt covered in
blood. I was sloppy, my hunger making me care-
less. There was no way I could stay the night at
the hotel. I would have to pack my things and
find another crossing point.

I drove slowly until I was out of the city then
sped back to the hotel. As my hunger subsided,
the guilt settled in. I killed two people. I wish I
could turn things back. I wish I could start it all
over again. But I couldn't. A glimmer of hope
pierced my darkness when I thought of Europe.
Maybe there was something going there that
would quell my hunger without taking anyone's
life. That was probably why they accepted our
kind. I wouldn't know until I got there.

I saw the commotion before I reached the hotel. The parking lot was filled with unmarked

cars. Inquisitors and clergy swarmed the parking lot, inspecting cars and knocking on doors. How did they find me so quickly? Did the clerk suspect something? It didn't matter. I had to run.

Something slammed into my car from behind. I didn't look to see; I just jumped out of my car and ran. Someone grabbed my arm and I struck out, hitting something hard. The person let go of me; I took a few more steps before I was tackled. I rolled and shoved the person off of me then clambered to my feet. A blinding pain flashed in my back and my limbs went limp. I collapsed to the ground; my vision blurred.

"We got her," I heard someone say.

"Let's get out of here before the others see us," another voice said.

"Hit her again," the first voice said.

Piercing pain swallowed me, and I blacked out.

* * *

I woke up in a white room strapped to a hospital bed raised to a sitting position. A gown covered my body and an IV was attached to my right arm. An Inquisitor stood at the door facing me; he frowned when he saw I was conscious then exited the room. I tugged at my restraints but I was strapped tight. A few minutes later the Inquisitor returned with another Inquisitor and a few others. Two were doctors, one an older woman with a graying afro and a suspicious grin, the other a tall man with short, cropped hair and a serious stare. The man carried a tablet; the woman went to the instruments and studied them.

"Well Miss Telisa, you've been a difficult person to find," the woman said. "I'm Dr. Felicia Garrett. My colleague is Dr. Samuel Phillips. It's an honor to finally meet a true vampire."

"Where are the clergy?" I asked.

"The clergy have nothing to do with this," Dr. Garrett replied. "This is a private operation."

"But the Inquisitors?"

"Holy Protectors in uniform only," the doctor replied. "They work for us."

"And who are you?" I asked.

"An interested party," Dr. Garrett replied. "You possess abilities that our clients are very interested in."

"I'm a vamp," I said. "There are plenty of us out there."

"But none quite like you," the doctor said. "You've developed a taste for human blood, thanks to your boyfriend."

My chest tightened.

"How . . . how is Kerry?" I asked.

"Kerry is dead," the doctor replied. "But you knew that, didn't you?"

I did, but to hear it crushed me. I held back my tears.

"But he didn't die in vain," the doctor continued. "He showed you what you are, and he showed us what you could become."

A nurse entered the room with an IV bag filled with a red fluid.

"No thanks," I said. "I already ate."

Dr. Garrett laughed aloud. Dr. Phillips smirked as he continued to type.

"Yes, you have," Dr. Garrett replied. "And you left quite a mess. Our people are still cleaning up."

The nurse replaced the IV drip the other bag.

"What is this?" I asked.

"It's a reunion of sorts," Dr. Garrett said. "You see, no other created vampire has reacted to human blood consumption like you. When given a choice, they do prefer human fluid, but they have no problem with blood fruit. But you crave it. We think it has everything to do with your relationship with Kerry."

"What are you saying?"

"He infected you," Dr. Garrett said. "But what he did to you was only partial."

The nurse began the drip.

"Today we see what happens with a total immersion. This serum was created from Kerry's blood. We found some interesting things in his genetic code, and you seem to be particularly sensitive to his . . . secretions."

"No . . . wait!" I yelled.

A burning sensation began where the IV needle pierced my skin then surged throughout my body. The pain became so intense I scream and convulsed, my arms and legs tugging at my straps. I felt like I was expanding like a balloon, growing so large that I was about to explode. Another scream escaped my mouth. The straps holding my arms snapped and I sat up. I looked down at Dr. Garrett and the others and saw their terror-filled eyes.

"Shoot her! Shoot her now!" Dr. Garrett screamed as she fled the room.

Through my agony I focused on the guards. Their faces were twisted by fear, and that pleased me. I yanked my legs free from the restraints before they could act then pounced at the guard to my right. He raised his lance and I batted it aside with my right hand then slammed my left hand into his throat. His eye bucked then closed as he slumped to the floor.

I looked at my hands. They were larger, with each of my elongated fingers tipped with talons. What had they done to me? I looked at my body and staggered. I was taller and thinner, yet hard muscles creased my skin. I dared not look at my face.

Something hit my chest and I staggered. I looked up to see the other fake Inquisitor aiming at me with his lance. I jumped the gap between us then stabbed my talons into his forehead. He dropped the lance as his arms fell to his side; his dead eyes locked on mine. I shook him free then tried to leave the room. Something held me back; I turned to see large wings protruding from my back. The sight made me weak and angry. Whatever they had done, they had turned me into a monster!

The rage consumed me again. I rampaged through the room, destroying everything in sight. I hunted for Dr. Garrett and her assistant, but they were nowhere to be seen. I had to get out. I had to get away. The room had no window, so I forced my way out the door and into the hallway.

The corridor was crammed with guards. They fired their lances, striking me all over my body with little effect. Whatever was done to me had made me stronger and seemingly invincible. I slice through them with my talons, hunting for the exit. When I finally find it, my way is clear except for a lone person standing in the way, Dr. Garrett. I run at her consumed with hate. She keeps her composure until I'm almost upon her, then her fear breaks through, radiating from her eyes. I grab her throat and lift her to eye level.

"What did you do to me?" I growl.

"It's the next step," she manages to say despite my grip on her neck. She jerked up her hand, holding a syringe filled with a fluid that looked similar to the one in the IV bag. I threw her into the wall before she could stab me and heard her head crack.

"There it is!"

I turned to see more guards running toward me. I ran out of the building into the night. Despite the darkness I could see like it was day. I sprinted across the parking lot too fast for them to catch up with me, so they began shooting. A bolt struck me in the back, knocking me off my feet. Instead of falling my wings extended and I glided back to my feet. Despite my better judgement I jump into the air.

"Fly," I whispered.

My wings flapped. I felt the muscles move that controlled them and I flapped harder and faster until I climbed up and over the trees surrounding the compound. There was nothing but forest below me; I had no idea where I was. I continued flying until I was far away from the compound, then I began looking for some kind of landmark to determine where I was. The lights from a large city emerged over the horizon, a glaring illumination due to my transformed eyesight. Once my eyes adjusted, I saw I was near Detroit. Before me was the narrow strip of water which separated the city from Windsor. It was not the way I planned to cross the border, but at that point it didn't matter. I flew into Canada and to freedom.

Days passed before I transformed into my normal self. I spent those days wandering the wilderness, feeding when I could and feeling remorse for every person I claimed. More days passed before my life returned to normal. Maria told me of a place I would be welcomed and she was right. They gave me clothes and a new identity. They also gave me blood. After a few more months I was ready to travel to Europe.

I roamed the continent for a time and eventually settled in Portugal. There were others like me . . . well, almost like me. I never told anyone about the transformations. Most of the time I can control it, but sometimes it takes over. At some point I need to seek help, but for the time being I have reveled in my solitude. I've heard there is a place in Uganda where there may be a 'cure' for our condition. They have a long history dealing with our kind, some say. For now, I'm content. In some ways I am free, and yet in other ways I will never be free again.

Initiation

(previously published in Blackened Roots: An Anthology of the Undead)

Maria watched the horde through her battered binoculars, searching for the perfect specimen. This was the third mass they had encountered since morning. The smell of decaying flesh reached them despite the distance, carried by a stiff wind which heralded an approaching rainstorm. She shifted her attention to the gathering clouds, lightning flashes proceeding the distant rumbles.

"You see one?" Leo asked.

Maria shifted her attention back to the hordes.

"Not yet," she replied.

The town had been ravaged by the undead before. Thinking beings would bypass it, but the hordes would sweep the same spots again and again.

Maria's eyebrows rose over the binocular lens.

"Got one!"

She focused on a smaller undead. It was probably eight or nine years old when it transitioned. The condition of its clothes indicated it had been taken recently. Maria stopped identifying them by gender long ago. The more you removed their humanity, the easier it was to do what you had to do to survive.

"Let's go," Leo said.

He started the motorcycle as she forced her helmet down over her voluminous afro then climbed into the sidecar. Leo drove slowly over the rough ground then accelerated when they reached the smoother asphalt. They covered half the distance before parking the bike. They were in no danger, but old habits were hard to break. Maria fished the shotgun from under their coats, and Leo grabbed the axe. They strolled across the patchwork of grass, weeds, and dirt as the undead entered the town. The creatures staggered in single file then separated, following the various streets branching from the main road.

The young one held back as if unsure, which was good for Leo and Maria. Maria opened the double barrel shotgun then inserted two buckshot shells. She crept closer until she was a meter away from it.

"Boo."

The undead turned and she pulled the trigger. The shot ripped through its head, sending decayed flesh and black blood everywhere. The headless creature tottered then fell forward.

Maria reloaded the shotgun as Leo strolled to the body.

"How much we need?" Maria asked.

"Not much."

Leo grabbed the undead's left arm and extended it. He chopped off the hand with one swing. It took three to cleave the arm at the elbow. He squatted before the body as Maria kept watch, picking up the arm and then putting it into a silk lined canvas bag.

"They're coming," Maria said. A gathering of undead walked toward them, blank eyes staring, deformed mouths open.

The duo strolled to the motorbike. Maria watched the group come closer and she smirked. Leo started the bike, but Maria raised her hand. "Wait," she said.

Leo frowned. "For what? We got what we came for."

"I want to see it work," she said.

Leo sighed then folded his arms on the bike handles. The undead came a few meters closer then stopped. They swayed in their unstable way, gazing around as if they could no longer see them. Then they turned away one by one, returning to the town.

Maria grinned. "Amazing." She hunkered down into the side car. "Let's go."

* * *

It was raining when they reached the compound. The tower guards recognized them and opened the gate a few minutes before they arrived. Camp folk waved as they sloshed by to the command tent in the center of the town. Leo stopped before the entrance and Maria climbed out of the sidecar, the canvas bag containing the arm parts slung over her shoulder.

"I'll meet you at home," she said.

Leo nodded then drove away. Maria watched him and warmth passed through her despite the cold drizzle. She was lucky. Leo was a good man. They had been through so much together since The Change, circumstances that would have destroyed most couples. But they survived. They found the commune and were accepted. Now they were contributing to the community in the most important way.

When she entered the tent, she was greeted by the stern face of Gretchen Moore, head scientist. The sepia colored clinic manager wore a dingy lab coat over her jeans and flannel shirt, her tight cross necklace barely visible. Maria threw up a lazy salute and Gretchen waved it off.

"Where's the package?" she said.

Maria handed her the bag. Gretchen opened it, looked inside then smiled.

"By Her Grace," she whispered. When she looked up, she radiated a reverent glow.

"You and Leo did an excellent job. I can see it's fresh. Did you watch the transformation?"

Maria barely hid her disgust. "No. It was travelling with the Pollo Horde," she answered.

Gretchen hurried away, Maria close behind. They pushed through the canvas curtain into her lab. Maria was always amazed at how clean she kept the facility. Gretchen sat the appendages on the lab table then went to her storage cabinet and took out a med kit. She gave it to Maria.

"Make sure his vitals are good," she said.

"I will," Maria replied.

"You must be excited."

"Actually, I'm a little scared."

Gretchen looked at her with wide eyes. "Scared? Why?"

Maria shrugged. "Old habits I guess."

Gretchen opened the bag. She took out the arm and admired it.

"You need to shake your doubts," Gretchen said. "Dr. Moore left us with an amazing legacy. It's terrible that he wasn't able to use it to save himself."

Gretchen closed her eyes then whispered a prayer. Everyone in the compound knew the story of Dr. Willis Moore and his revolutionary discovery. It was his serum that made life in the compound possible. It was also his search to improve his discovery that led him to become what he fought to destroy.

When Gretchen opened her eyes, the serious expression had returned.

"Make sure you check Barron's vitals. We need him in his best shape for Initiation."

"I will," Maria replied. "Thank you, Gretchen."

"No need to thank me. We are Tribe."

"We are Tribe," Maria repeated.

Maria left the med tent then hurried home. Leo's bike was parked out front, covered with a rain canvas. As she entered the tent, she saw her men sitting at the rusted folding table enjoying bowls of bone soup. Barron looked up and his face glowed.

"Mami!"

He jumped from his seat, then wrapped her in a crushing loving hug. He was almost as tall as Leo now, which made her happy and sad. She was gaining a healthy man but losing her boy.

"Let your mother go so she can eat," Leo said playfully.

They walked together to the table, separating to sit. The bone soup was warm and soothing.

"What did Gretchen say?" Leo asked.

"Everything is good," Maria replied. "Initiation is on schedule."

Barron's face dimmed; his smile replaced by a nervous scowl. Maria reached out and touched his hand.

"It's nothing to worry about," she said. "Everything will be fine."

"I'm not worried about that," Barron replied. "I'm nervous about the ceremony. I don't like crowds."

"I know," Leo said. "But Initiation is important to Tribe and us. It's the reason we still exist while others have perished."

"Plus it doesn't last long," Maria said in a soothing tone. "And when it's over, you can finally leave the compound."

Barron's nervousness subsided. "That would be great!"

"Now let's finish this delicious soup. I need to check your vitals," Maria said.

Barron lowered his spoon. "Why?"

"You have to be at your healthiest to participate in Initiation."

"I feel good," Barron said.

"Of course, you do. You're my son," Maria said. "But that's not enough for Gretchen. She needs her stupid numbers."

They finished their meal. Leo collected their bowls then carried them to the water bucket for washing. Barron was standing to leave the table when Maria waved him down.

"No you don't, young man." She lifted the test kit. "Remember?"

Barron frowned then plopped onto his seat. Maria broke the seal on the kit then opened it. Inside was a thermometer, stethoscope, blood pressure cuff, and a blood sample kit. The faded instructions were tucked under the instruments. Maria unfolded them then read them. She knew them by heart, but it never hurt to read them again just in case Gretchen made any changes.

"Okay young man let's do this," she said.

Barron passed the tests with no problem. The only variable was the blood sample analysis. She would have to wait for Gretchen for those results.

"So, am I alive?" Barron asked.

"No," Maria replied. "We'll have to kick you out of the compound to roam around with your friends."

"That's not funny," Barron said.

Maria hugged him. "After initiation you won't have to worry about that ever again."

* * *

The following weeks were spent in preparation of Initiation. Teams scoured the nearby ruins and abandoned homes for items and trinkets for the ceremony. The city blacksmiths converted those objects into jewelry for the initiates and their families. None of this was necessary, but the town leaders understood how important celebration and recognition was to the survivors. Maria went to the seamstress to have Leo's initiation jacket resized for Barron, who was already bigger and broader than his father. After initiation, he would be a valuable addition to the tribe. Maria couldn't help but smile.

The night finally arrived. A full moon lay its muted light on the compound, illuminating the celebrants as they made their way to Town Center. The moonglow was gradually usurped by the bonfire light, the blazing pile of hardwood and incense sending smoke and fragrance into the clear night sky.

Barron put on his jacket then buttoned it as Maria and Leo watched. He looked up at them both, a nervous smile on his face.

"So, I guess this is it," he said.

"It is," Maria replied.

He stood and Maria hugged him tight then kissed his forehead.

"Everything will be fine," she whispered.

Maria stepped away and watched Leo embrace him.

"See you on the other side," he said.

They picked up their instruments. Maria's tambourine was weathered but still useful. Leo's shaker gourd was missing a few beads but still sang with every motion. They could hear the drumming inside their tent, so they played in syncopation.

"Lead the way, son," Maria said.

Barron danced out the tent in time with the rhythm flowing throughout the compound. Maria and Leo followed, matching their steps with the drums. They joined the other families prancing their way to Center, some with initiates, some without, but everyone joyful. As they reached the center, Maria and Leo joined the ring of parents and relatives of the initiates. Behind them stood the other tribe members, their expressions just as joyful as the parents. New initiates meant new hope for a better future.

Standing before the bonfire was Gretchen. The cold expression and clinical clothing were gone, replaced by a hand woven woolen dress that fell from her shoulders to her ankles to rest on the insteps of her bare feet. A mural decorated the garment, an abstract story of the tribe, from its founding to the present day. As far as they knew, they were the only humans thriving in this new world. It was because of the gift bestowed on them decades ago, a protection that would now be given to their new initiates.

Standing on either side of Gretchen were her acolytes, people chosen for training so that one day they would take her place. They wore wooden masks with slits to represent their eyes and mouth. Black robes covered their bodies and they too were shoeless. Each held a large gourd in their left hands, a small cup in their right.

The initiates walked in time with the pulsing music until they reached Gretchen and the acolytes. Maria reached out and grasped Leo's hand and they shared a smile. They watched Barron turn to his right, walking a few paces then stopping just beyond the acolytes. Once the others were in place, they swayed in time with Gretchen and the acolytes. Gretchen raised her arms; she let them drop and the drumming ceased. The camp fell silent.

"Tribe!" she shouted. "What are we?"

"We are one!" Maria shouted with the others.

"Tribe!" she shouted again. "What are we?"

"We are one!" they responded.

Gretchen began pacing.

"Forty years ago, we were blessed," she said. "A man who owed us nothing gave us everything. Since that day we have prospered, able to live free of the plague that possesses others. His only demand of us was to share with others, to one day make the world free as it once was."

Gretchen turned her back to Maria and the other parents to face the new initiates.

"You have been among the Tribe since the day you were born. Tonight, you become a part of the Tribe. From this day forward you will share our responsibility upon your shoulders. But do not worry. We are here to love, nurture and support you."

Gretchen took the large gourd from the acolyte on her right.

"Kneel," she commanded.

Maria's throat went dry. Barron knelt with the others then glanced back at her. He smiled nervously.

"Hold out your hands," Gretchen ordered.

Barron returned his attention to Gretchen, holding out his hands. The second acolyte gave each initiate a cup which Gretchen filled from her gourd. Maria grimaced as she remembered drinking that same concoction. It was nasty but necessary for what was to come. The others watched with the same remembrance, spouting encouragements to the initiates as they forced the drink down.

Gretchen waited until the final initiate finished before signaling the first acolyte. They brought her a worn leather case, the same case that once held the first vials of the lifesaving serum. The acolyte followed Gretchen to the first initiate and opened the case. Gretchen took out the needle, swabbed the initiate's arm the administered the shot.

"Haynes!" she called out.

Doretha and Samuel Haynes hurried to the circle, catching their daughter before she collapsed. The others cheered as they led her away to their home to recover from the inoculation. Maria barely heard the other names announced as she watched Barron waiting his turn. After what seemed like an eternity, she heard Gretchen call out their name. Leo was already on his feet and making his way to the inner circle. Maria pursued him, her face hot with emotion. They reached Barron at the same time, wrapping him up like a winter's blanket. Barron looked at them with bleary eyes, grinning through the obvious pain.

"I did it," he whispered.

Maria kissed his cheek. "Yes, you did. Now let's get you home."

They carried their son home amid the yells of praise and celebration, his burden easing as he regained his strength. By the time they reached their tent he was almost walking on his own.

"I'm okay," he said.

"No, you're not," Leo replied. "You just think you are."

"I feel fine," Barron argued.

"Trust us, son," Maria said. "We've done this a few times. Everybody feels okay until they fall flat on their face. Let's avoid that broken nose."

Barron shrugged and allowed them to take him to his cot. As they eased him down, he swooned. Maria steadied him.

"Wow. Wasn't expecting that," Barron said.

Maria grinned. "See? Let's ease you back on this cot."

Maria and Leo lowered Barron onto his thin mattress. He closed his eyes and sighed.

"This feels good."

"Keep an eye on him," Maria said to Leo. "I'm going to brew some soup."

"I'm not hungry," Barron said.

"You will be," Maria replied.

She went outside and started a fire then went to the well for water. Going back into the tent for soup bones and herbs, she saw Leo hovering over Barron. Relief washed over her as she returned to the fire with her cooking pot. Their boy was safe now, able to travel anywhere without fear. Once they were sure he was fully immune they would do what they always planned; leave the Tribe. Without the zombie threat there was no reason for them to stay.

Maria finished the soup. She filled the stone bowl then took it inside. Barron was sitting up. He smiled when he saw her and licked his lips. Maria laughed.

"Told you you'll be hungry."

She handed him the bowl and he looked at its contents and frowned.

"That's all?"

"You're not ready for solid food yet," Maria said. "But you can have all the soup you can eat."

"Yeah, it's not like it's going to stay around long," Leo said.

Barron's eyes widened. "What are you talking about?"

"You'll see."

Maria and Leo nursed Barron through the night. By morning he finally slept, and they did, too. Maria was the first to wake up early that afternoon. She rummaged through their stock for a few items to trade then hurried to the central market, returning home with bread, a freshly dressed chicken, and a few potatoes. Leo was cleaning the tent when she entered. Barron sat on the edge of his cot, a tired look in his eyes.

"Is it over yet?" he asked.

"You tell us," Maria said. "How do you feel?"

"Like I've been hit by a hammer," Barron said.

"You're better then," Maria said. "It will take at least three days. Your body is going through profound changes. Once it's done, you'll be like us. You'll be able to go anywhere."

"How soon?" Barron asked.

"Two weeks at the most," Maria said. "Then when you're rested, we'll take you Out."

Barron's eyes lit up. "Finally!"

"Calm down," Maria said. "Going Out is not an adventure. It's essential work. And despite your vaccination, it's still dangerous. There are other monsters to deal with."

"Other monsters?"

Barron's worried look made Maria wished she hadn't mentioned it. She patted his shoulder.

"Don't worry about that. It's nothing we can't manage."

Maria and Leo resumed their duties with each taking turns with Barron. Twelve days after the initiation he was fully recovered and ready for his first trip Outside. Maria bartered with other villagers to get him the proper gear. Leo found him a twelve gauge shotgun in good condition, something that would keep him safe while not requiring accuracy. Though Barron had taken shooting like others in the camp, there was a huge difference between shooting targets and a real firefight.

Maria woke Barron that morning with a gentle nudge.

"Come on, villager," she whispered. "It's time."

Barron sprang up, almost bumping heads with Maria.

"Calm down!" she said. "Let's eat breakfast then head out."

They sat at the table, eating oatmeal and dried beef before getting their gear. Leo inspected Barron.

"Remember to stay close to us," he said. "Our sweep is going to take us to an area where the undead wander."

Barron's eye went wide. "Why?"

"We need to make sure your protected," Maria replied. "This is the only way to find out."

"But what if they're too many?"

"We're travelling with the other initiates," Leo said. "They'll be enough of us to make sure nothing happens."

Leo stood back from Barron then smiled.

"You're as ready as you're ever going to be."

"Good," Maria replied. "Let's go."

They met the other families outside the town gates then proceeded on their sweep. The Haynes led the trek, their daughter walking timidly between her parents. Maria, Leo, and Barron brought up the rear.

"Why are we in the back?" Barron asked.

"It's just as important to keep an eye on where we've been as it is observing where we're going."

"Will the undead try to sneak up on us?" Barron asked.

Leo shook his head. "They're not that clever. It's the others we're concerned about. The others like us."

"Other people? Why?"

Maria draped her arm on Barron's shoulders.

"You have lived a privileged life, especially during these times. We were lucky to find Tribe; it was even luckier that they accepted us. They shared the Gift with us, and everything else. We have crops and livestock. What we can't make, we scavenge from the nearby towns. Others are not so fortunate. They fend for themselves, living off what they can find, or what they can take."

"Like the undead?" he asked.

"Something like that, except they live and breathe like us."

Barron looked thoughtful for a moment.

"Why don't we just share with them?"

Maria sighed. "We tried, but there's something about people in times of scarcity. Some see generosity as weakness. It's also why the founders set up our town among the undead. They can't reach us here. But we can reach them."

"Are they our enemies?"

Maria shrugged. "They're certainly not our friends."

"Initiates!"

Carla Haynes's call ended their conversation. Maria and Leo followed Barron to the others. Carla stood at the top of a steep hill. She waved everyone up. They saw the wrecked city in the valley below, a dilapidated sprawl bordering a wide river. There was movement between the structures.

"Looks like a horde," she said to Maria as she handed her the binoculars. "A good time to confirm."

Maria's hand shook as she handed the binoculars back. Carla shared a reassuring smile.

"It's just routine," she said. "You should know."

"Yeah, but he's still my son."

"And Jennette is still my daughter," Carla said. "We have to confirm."

Carla didn't wait for Maria's or any of the other parents' approval. She didn't need it.

"Initiates!"

The new citizens gathered around her.

"We're going into that town. We've spotted undead inside. You're taking the lead."

The young initiates looked at each other then their parents. Maria forced a smile as she looked at Barron.

"It's okay," she said. "We'll be close behind. There's nothing to worry about."

Barron smiled and nodded. He cocked his pump action shotgun then stepped forward. Maria wondered if the confident look on his face was real or bravado. The other initiates fell in with him, their eyes on him. He was taking the leadership among them, which was good.

"Spread out," Carla said. "Make a single line and approach slowly."

The initiates did as ordered, Barron in the center. They marched toward the city, guns ready. Maria and Leo formed another line with the parents and other expedition members, keeping a few meters behind them. The closer they came to the city without incident, the better Maria felt. The undead didn't sense them. The serum injected into all of them rendered them invisible, because they emitted the same odors of the undead. Smell was the primary sense of the unfortunate dead, all other senses secondary.

Carla raised her binoculars, then jerked them down.

"Stop!" she shouted.

Maria rushed to her side. "What's wrong?"

"They're coming."

"What?"

"They're coming!"

"Everyone fall back!" Maria shouted.

"Wait," Carla said. "We must do this the right way. Some of the initiates' serum didn't take. We need to know who."

"What are you saying?"

"We pull them back one by one."

"That's crazy!"

"We can't jeopardize the safety of Tribe," Carla said. Maria wanted to protest, but she knew Carla was right. They had to know.

"Initiates!" Carla called out. "Stay where you are. Pull back beyond the second line when your name is called."

Maria took her place beside Leo while Carla called out the initiates' name. With each call, the undead continued to advance. Maria checked her rifle over and over as they came closer, her eyes fixed on Barron. The last initiates remaining were Barron and Michelle Haynes. The undead continued to come.

"Barron!" Carla shouted.

Maria watched as Barron touched Michelle's shoulder then whispered in her ear. He backed away until he was behind and beyond the second line. The undead slowed, then stopped.

"Oh God!" Maria said. She broke the line, running to Barron with Leo close behind.

"Let's go now!" she said.

Barron was dumbfounded.

"Mama, what's going on?"

"Let's go son," Leo said.

Maria grabbed Barron's arm then led him away. The trio marched nonstop back to the compound in silence, each of them caught up in their own thoughts. The guards let them enter, curiosity evident on their faces. They didn't stop until they were inside their tent.

"Mama, what's wrong?" Barron asked.

Maria couldn't answer. She looked at Leo then dropped her face into her hands.

"Son," Leo began, "when Carla called you back to the line, the undead stopped their advance."

Barron eyes went wide. "What does that mean?"

"It means your shot didn't take," Leo replied. "See, the serum makes us invisible to the undead by incorporating part of them into us. When they sense us, they sense their own. It's how we can live here, how we thrive without fear of them. Since your serum didn't take, the undead could possibly find you here. They could find the entire compound."

Barron sat hard. "Oh."

Maria lifted her head and watched Barron's eyes dart between her and Leo.

"Will they make us leave?" Barron asked.

Leo began to answer, but Maria stopped him with a headshake.

"We don't know," she said. "We'll have to wait and see."

"But if I'm a threat to Tribe . . ."

"Let's just wait," Maria said.

The rest of the patrol arrived at the compound at dusk. Maria, Leo, and Barron were eating their evening meal when Carla entered their tent. She scanned with a sympathetic gaze before speaking.

"Maria, Leo. Let's talk outside."

They followed her out of the tent.

"You saw what we all saw," Carla said. "Best you do what you need to do on your own and don't make a big scene about it. You've been here a long time, and everyone loves you, but you know how important it is that we keep Tribe pure."

"No," Maria said.

Carla sighed. "Come on, Maria. I hate this as much as you do."

"No, you don't," Maria replied. "It's not your child. I want to talk to Gretchen. I want Barron to take another shot. Maybe Gretchen got it wrong."

"She didn't," Carla replied. "He was the only initiate the undead responded to."

"I don't care. I want Gretchen to give him another shot!"

Maria pushed by Carla, striding to Gretchen's clinic. She ignored the receptionist's efforts to stop her, stomping through the narrow hall until she reached the office. Gretchen sat at her desk as if expecting her.

"I knew you would come," Gretchen said.
"Carla informed me before she went to you."

"Give him another shot," Maria said.

"It won't do any good," Gretchen replied.

"How do you know?" Carla asked. "Have you done it before?"

Gretchen shifted in her chair as if she sat on a tack.

"No, but . . ."

"Then do it now," Maria said. "As much as Leo and I have done for you, we owe us that."

"It's not that simple," Gretchen replied. "It took years and lives to develop the serum. The body can tolerate one dose. Anything beyond that can cause unexpected consequences."

"Do you know this for a fact?" Maria asked.

"No, but the doctor's notes are thorough. I have no reasons to doubt him."

Maria dropped into chair before Gretchen's desk.

"Please, Gretchen," she said. "I can't have Barron living like this, constantly fearing those things. I have to try. We have to try."

"It's not so bad," Gretchen said. "You can stay with Tribe. I'll push through a waiver. It's no reason we have to be as rigid as we were in the past. But Barron can never leave the compound again."

"I can't have him live a life like that without trying," Maria replied. "Please, Gretchen. Please."

Gretchen steepled her fingers, a distant look on her face.

"If it works, it will be a breakthrough," she said.

"It will work," Maria replied.

Gretchen finally looked at Maria.

"Get me another specimen," she said. "Something fresh."

Maria jumped to her feet. "Yes! I'll go now."

"He'll have to be quarantined in the clinic until the symptoms subside," Gretchen said.

"Of course," Maria replied.

She worked her way around the desk then wrapped Gretchen in a tight hug.

"Thank you."

Maria hurried out of the clinic. Leo and Barron jumped to their feet when she entered the tent.

"Grab your gear, Leo. We're going for a specimen."

"What about me?" Barron said.

Maria went to Barron, placing her hands on his cheeks.

"You're going to be all right. Stay in the tent and don't let anyone in until we return. Understand?

"Yes, Mama."

She kissed him then left the tent. Carla met her outside.

"Where are you going?"

"Back to the city for a specimen."

"So, Gretchen agreed to try again?"

"Yes."

"I'm coming with you."

Maria stopped then spun around.

"No, you're not. A few minutes ago, you were ready to kick us out. We don't need your help."

"It wasn't personal," Carla replied. "The Tribe comes first. What you're doing might save others."

"Fuck the Tribe," Maria said. "I'm doing this for my son. If I see you following us, I swear to God I'll blow your brains out."

Maria stomped away before Carla could respond. She was out the gate and crossing the protective clearing when Leo caught up with her.

"What's the plan?"

"We go back to the city, snatch an undead, get our specimen and come back."

Leo looked around. "It's dusk. We should probably wait until morning."

"Either help me or go back," Maria said.

"I'm with you, you know that," Leo said. "It's just . . ."

"It's our son, Leo! Our son!"

Leo looked away. "You're right. Let's go."

They hurried over the rough terrain, reaching the town as the last sunlight trickled below the western horizon.

"We can't go in after dark; you know that right?"

"I know," Maria said. "We'll lure them out here."

"With what?"

Maria reached into her bag then took out a large flashlight. No one in the compound knew she owned it; if they did, it would be confiscated by camp enforcers. She was lucky to have discovered batteries that still held a charge, which she never used unless in emergencies. Leo looked at the light and said nothing.

Maria turned on the light. The beam illuminated a small area just outside the town's outskirts.

"We're not close enough," she said.

They gathered their gear and moved closer until the light revealed the damaged building walls. Leo aimed his rifle in the direction of the light, his face tense. Maria flashed the light off and on for an hour before spotting movement.

"Something's coming," she said.

Leo raised his rifle to his shoulder. Maria let the light stream as the undead emerged from the dilapidated structures, trudging in its rambling way.

"Looks like one so far," Leo said.

"All we need," Maria replied.

They walked toward the being, closing the gap quickly. They were with killing range when Maria held up her hand. More undead stumbled from the building. Maria turned off the light.

"Can't see well," Leo said.

"Shoot where it was," Maria replied.

Leo aimed then fired. The rifle report echoed across the dark emptiness and the distance hills. Maria flashed the light; the undead lay in the grass, its body twitching in a second death. Leo took out machete, Maria her shotgun. Leo made quick work of the carcass, chopping the arm free then wrapping it in canvas as Maria watched the other undead.

"Let's go."

They trotted away, Maria looking behind them. The other undead milled around their victim, some staring blankly at the body, others looking into the darkness. The grim scene faded as they crested the hill then descended into the expanse leading to the compound. The gate was secured; Maria pounded it until the sentries let them in.

"Go get Barron," Maria said. "I'm headed to the clinic."

Maria was sure Gretchen was asleep, but she didn't care. She banged on the door until the doctor answered. Gretchen looked disgruntled as she let Maria in, but she didn't protest. She went to the lab and prepared the instruments; Maria took out the appendage and placed it on the table.

"It will take a few hours to prepare the vaccine," Gretchen said as she worked.

"I'll wait," Maria replied.

Maria walked to the waiting room. Leo and Barron arrived a few minutes later. Barron, his eyes heavy with worry and fatigue, managed to smile before plopping onto a seat and falling back to sleep. Leo sat beside Maria.

"Get some sleep," he said. "I'll take first watch."

"I can't," she said. "Not until Barron gets the vaccine. You go ahead."

Leo settled, slumping into his chair and immediately falling asleep. Maria watched them both, her eyes damp. She loved them without bounds. She couldn't image being without either of them.

Sleep slowly overwhelmed her despite her diligence.

"Maria."

Maria sat upright, looking about to find Gretchen's serious face.

"It's done. Let's get Barron prepped."

Maria woke Barron. He stood without question then followed them into the office. Gretchen motioned to the chair and Barron sat and rolled up his sleeve. Gretchen administered the shot quickly.

"Same instructions as before," she said. "Take him home and let him rest. He might have a slight fever and fatigue. When the fever breaks, bring him back."

Maria hugged Gretchen. "Thank you for doing this."

"Don't thank me yet," Gretchen said. "We still have to take him out again once he's recovered to make sure it took. You can thank me then."

Maria led Barron back to their tent. He lay in his bed, a hopeful smile on his face.

"It will be okay, Mama," he said. "This time will take."

Maria shared a smile she didn't feel. "I know baby. Just rest. I'll be right here."

The days passed and Maria stayed. Barron's symptoms came, and she did what she could. Leo watched over both of them, making sure they ate and helping Maria when she needed to rest or relieve herself. The compound took on an eerie silence despite everyone going about their routines, each person concerned about Barron's condition. But like Maria, all they could do was wait.

Seven days after the re-inoculation, Maria awoke during the night. She was thirsty, her mouth dry from sleeping with it open. She had no doubt been snoring, something Leo accused her of for years which she denied. She decided to check on Barron. He was still, his eyes wide.

"Barron?"

Maria shook him and he didn't respond.

"Barron!"

She grabbed his shoulders, staring in into his blank orbs. Leo came behind her.

"What's going on?"

Maria turned to him, tearing running from her eyes.

"He's dead!"

Leo moved her aside, pressing his fingers against his neck. He jerked his hand away then grabbed Maria, pulling her back.

"He's not dead," he said.

Maria glared at him. "What do you mean he's not dead?"

Leo laid his hand on her shoulders. "We have to get him out of here. Now."

"What the fuck are you talking about? What are you . . ."

She saw the answer in Leo's eyes. Her arms dropped to her side, and she turned around. "Oh God. Oh God no."

Barron's eyes focused on her. There was no emotion, no recognition.

"Help me," Leo said.

Maria couldn't move. She watched Leo take rope from their storage chest then use it to tie Barron's arms to his torso and secure his ankles. He went back to the chest and returned with a canvas bag that he draped over his head then tied shut.

"Help me lift him," he said.

Maria leaned for Barron but as she reached out to touch him, she found her hands frozen. She looked up into Leo's eyes.

"I . . . I can't . . . It's my . . ."

Leo touched her cheek. "It's okay. I'll do it."

He cradled Barron into his arms then maneuvered him over his shoulder. Maria hurried to the tent flap then opened it.

"We'll need horses," he said.

"I'll get them," Maria replied.

She ran to the stables, staying as quiet as she could manage. The compound was asleep; even the guards had dozed off. She saddled two of the most docile horses then led them to the tent. Both pulled back when she neared Leo and Barron. Maria patted them as she struggled not to break down. Leo lifted Barron onto the mare then climbed onto the saddle. Maria mounted the other horse, and they rode to the gate. As they neared it, they saw a person standing in the middle of the road holding a shotgun.

"Gretchen," Maria whispered.

She ambled to them. "You should end it here," she said.

"Get out of the way," Maria replied.

"What are you going to do?" Gretchen asked. "Set him free? To what?"

"We'll do what we have to do," Leo said. "But not here."

Gretchen nodded. She went to the gate then opened it.

"I'm sorry," she said. "I hoped it would work."

"Me, too," Maria replied.

Once they were a distance away from camp they urged the horses to a gallop, riding hard until they reached the river and the old town. Leo climbed down from his horse then lowered Barron to the ground. He untied his arms and legs then removed the bag.

"Let's go," he said.

"No," Maria replied. "Let's wait."

Together they watched for the inevitable. After an hour Barron, or what used to be Barron, sat up then struggled to his feet. He turned to them; his eyes locked on Maria.

"Give me something," she whispered. "Let me know you're still there."

But there was nothing left. Barron turned then staggered away toward the river. The tears came hard as she reached for her rifle then took aim.

"I'm so sorry," she said. "I love you. I always will."

She pulled the trigger.

Why Petey Came Back

They laid Petey Cole to rest on a sunny Sunday morning at Big Bethel AME Church in Harris County. Reverend Charley Mitchell presided over the homegoing ceremony, and most of Petey's family was in attendance. There was a fine repast afterward that became sort of a family reunion with relatives coming from as far as Ekleta, Alabama. Death has a way of bringing kinfolks together like that.

Eight days later old Petey dug himself out of that five-hundred-dollar pinewood casket and through six feet of red clay, rising up a lot dirty and a little ripe. Why? Because Petey had unfinished business, and he was never a man to leave loose ends.

Petey surveyed his surroundings with a bad attitude. He had no illusions. A few minutes ago, he was as dead as a slow armadillo crossing an eight-lane highway. But the good Lord above gave Petey a little more time because the circumstances of his demise deserved some recompense. The only problem with being dead is that the body had commenced to become one with the earth. The crackles shaking his legs as he stood told him that he only had so much time to do what he had to do, so he needed help. There was only one person that Petey could depend on no matter what, at least when he was alive. And it was his good fortune that that person lived a few miles away from the cemetery. So Petey set his hips as good as he could and stumbled his way to Xavier Johnson's apartment on Buena Vista Road.

Xavier lay sprawled on his air mattress, deep in intoxicated bliss. The temp job he landed two weeks ago provided enough for him to pay his bills and have a little left over for a few indulges. When Petey died he didn't know how he was gonna make it. Petey was always good for work when a brother needed it, legal or otherwise, and he paid well under the table. The tears he shed at his friend's funeral were more for himself than grief.

The urgent knocking on his door pissed him off. He reached for the baseball bat he kept beside the mattress before answering.

"Who the hell is it?"

"Zee! Get yo' ass up and answer the damn door!"

Xavier bolted upright like somebody shoved a stick up his ass. His hands trembled before he spoke again.

"Petey?"

"Who else would it be?"

Terror swept through Xavier, quickly followed by rage. Who was acting like his dead boy? He jumped off the mattress, stomping to the door with the bat raised high in his right hand. He undid the four latches, unlocked the door handle then snatched the door wide.

"Who the . . ."

Petey stood before him, his death suit stained with Georgia red clay, his skin sagging on his face and smelling like a full dumpster in the middle of the summer. Xavier's mind went blank as he collapsed.

Petey caught Xavier and carried him to his mattress. He dropped him and then surveyed the room, shaking his head. He'd only been dead little over a week and Zee was already struggling. He tried to teach him the business, but some people were just meant to be the help. And with Zee's reputation, not too many folks would want his help.

"Wake up, man!" Petey said. "We got work to do, and not a lot of time to do it."

He shook Zee again and his right middle finger fell off.

"Shit! Come on, Zee!"

Zee's eyes cracked open. They focused on Petey's decaying face and rolled up.

"Lawd Jesus!"

Zee began going limp in Petey's arms but Petey wasn't having it.

"Hell naw, bruh. Wake yo' ass up. I need you."

Zee began struggling. "Why you here man? You supposed to be dead!"

"I know," Petey replied. "But I got something to take care of and you're gonna help me. You know how I am about my business."

Xavier pushed away from Petey. "Why I got to help you? Can't you find somebody already dead to do it?"

"I'm not that dead, at least not yet," Petey replied.

Xavier began blinking.

"What the hell you doing?" Petey asked.

"Trying to wake up," Xavier said. "This ain't nothing but a fucked-up dream!"

Petey sighed and three teeth fell out of his mouth. Time was running out.

"Yeah, this is a dream," Petey said. "And the only way you can wake up is to help me."

Xavier stopped blinking. "For real?"

"For real."

"Okay," Xavier said. "What I got to do?"

"You got a gun?"

"You sure you Petey, 'cause Petey would know I'm scared of guns."

"That's right," Petey said. "Because of your mama."

Xavier's eyes closed for a second. "My sweet mama."

Xavier's expression became serious. "What's my favorite color?"

"What?"

Xavier's hands clenched. "What's my favorite color?"

"How the hell I'm supposed to know!?!"

"If you were Petey, you would know."

"No I wouldn't! I wasn't your damn friend!"

Xavier grinned. "You Petey all right! So why you in my dream?"

"That don't matter," Petey said. "I need a pistol. Where can I get one?"

Xaiver's eyes narrowed. "You know where to go. You just don't want to . . . because you're scared."

"I ain't . . ."

But he was. There was only one person on the streets that Petey wouldn't mess with, and that was Dirty Red. The man didn't care about nothing and nobody and would shoot you without blinking an eye. But that wasn't a concern anymore.

"Either take me there or give me directions," he finally said.

"You sure?"

Petey laughed. "What's Dirty Red gonna do to me? Shit, I'm already dead."

"I ain't though," Xavier replied. "And since I ain't sure this a dream or not, I'm a write them directions for you."

Zee shuffled over to his bed then went into a large duffle bag resting beside it. He took out a pencil and a notepad then scribbled Dirty Red's address and gave it to Petey.

"Where your keys?"

"Now hold up," Xavier said. "I'm your boy, but I don't let just anybody drive my ride."

"Then you gonna take me."

Something must have snapped in Xavier right about then. His eyes narrowed and he spit on the floor.

"I ain't doing a damn thing! This is my dream, and I'm tired of you telling me what to do. Get your ass back to that damn hole in the gr . . ."

Petey slapped Xavier as hard as he could. He heard a loud snap then looked at his right arm. It bent the wrong way between his wrist and his elbow. The bone stuck out the skin.

"Damn," he said.

Xavier was laid out on his back, eyes closed. A few seconds later his eyelids fluttered then rose. He sat up, then rubbed his cheek.

"This ain't no dream, is it?"

"Naw, it ain't," Petey said. "Now get yo' ass up and take me to Dirty Red's."

Xavier went into his bag again and got his keys. He shivered as he walked past Petey and out the door. Petey followed Xavier around the back of the apartments to a narrow alleyway. Parked next to the clothesline was a sky-blue Galaxie 500.

"Nice ride," Petey said.

"Thank you," Xavier answered. "I stole it last week. Figure I got about two more weeks before I have to ditch it."

"I'll get in the back," Petey said.

Petey opened the door and struggled into the back seat. He was getting weaker; time was not on his side.

"Make it quick Zee," he said.

Xavier made a bee line to Dirty Red's café. The small juke joint was a cover for his real business, fencing stolen goods. Just inside of the door were two guards sitting in the last booth closest to the jukebox, Bo and Jimmy. Xavier parked as close as he could to the door.

"You want me to go in?" Xavier asked.

"Naw," Petey replied. "Bo and Jimmy would beat your ass and toss you out."

"They'll do the same to you," Xavier replied.

"I don't think so."

Xavier got out of the car and opened the door for Petey. Petey straightened himself up the best a dead man in a dirty suit could then walked as steady as his failing legs would allow. He pushed the swing door open so hard it slammed against the wall.

"Dirty Red! Where you at?"

Bo and Jimmy dropped their playing cards then jumped to their feet. They were rolling up their sleeves to give Petey a good ass whupping when they recognized who it was. Bo just ran out the door. Jimmy stood frozen.

"Got damn! Petey done came back!" He crumpled to the floor.

The shot filled the juke joint. Petey stumbled backward then caught the doorframe. The second shot hit him in the gut and he bent over from the force. There was no pain; why would there be? The third shot grazed his head, knocking his head around so far, he could see behind him. He reached up with both hands and turned it back around. Dirty Red stood there, a wet spot between his legs, his mouth agape. Petey smiled.

"That's some good shooting. Real good. I came here for a pistol. I think I'll take that one."

Petey sauntered up to Dirty Red. The gangster flinched as Petey grasped his hand, then pried Red's fingers from around the nickel-plated .357 revolver. Petey hefted the gun.

"Should be three more rounds in it. Two more than I need. Thank you, brother."

Petey ambled toward the door, wet stains forming where the bullets struck him. Something ran from his scalp too, but he didn't have time to check. He turned back around to see Dirty Red still frozen in place, eyes locked on him, teeth chattering.

"Looks like I scared the piss out of him."

Petey's laugh echoed in the juke joint as he walked out the door. He was stumbling down the steps when Xavier pulled up, slammed on the brakes then jumped out of the car to let Petey in. He shoved Petey inside the car, scurried back to the driver's side then sped off.

"I heard shooting!" Xavier said. He glanced at the gun in Petey's hand then looked forward. "You shoot him?"

"Naw. He shot me. Three times."

"So you really is dead."

"And you really are stupid."

"Where we going now?"

"To Lucy's."

Xavier swerved into a right turn, throwing Petey into the driver's side window. He slammed on the brakes and Petey bounced off the back of the front seat.

"Man, what's wrong with you?"

"What's wrong with you?" Xavier shouted back. "Bad enough that you ain't dead and come to haunt me. Now you want to get Lucy, too?"

"Just drive, Zee."

"No," Xavier said. "I ain't letting nothing happen to Lucy."

Petey blacked out for a second. His time was drifting away.

"I ain't gonna hurt Lucy," Petey replied. "I'm trying to save her life."

Xavier turned around. "What?"

"Lucy's old man has been beating her," Petey said. "She came to work one day all bruised up. It's been happening for a while now, but I figured it was none of my business. But this time it was bad. Real bad. I told her I'd fix things, but she told me it was okay. But it wasn't. So I took it on myself to set things straight. Showed up at his job on the docks and told him if he hit Lucy one more time, he was gonna end up looking worse than her. He called himself pushing up on me, so I gave him a preview. I thought that was the end of it, but I underestimated him."

Petey turned his head around and showed Xavier the dent in his skull.

"That wasn't no accident," he said. "Son of a bitch broke into my house and was waiting for me. Busted my skull when I got to the top of the stairs. I guess he figured folks would think I fell. He was right."

Petey checked the .357 again. "Now it's payback time."

The smile faded from Xavier's face. "Damn right it is."

Petey didn't have to tell Xavier how to get to Lucy's crib; he'd driven her home from work a few times. He parked his car far enough away not to be noticed but close enough to see. An hour passed before the front door opened and Lucy emerged, followed by her old man. They got into her Malibu then drove away.

"Let's go," Petey said.

Xavier drove by the house then parked. He got out of the car then snuck to the back. A few minutes later he opened the front door. Petey dragged himself out the Galaxie then trudged inside.

"Get that chair and set it over there," Petey said. Xavier moved the chair directly in front of the door.

"Now go," Petey said.

"You sure?" Xavier asked. "You don't look so good."

Xavier laughed then went into of fit of coughing. Black ichor seeped from his mouth.

"Go on back," he said. "I got this."

Xavier locked the front door then exited out the back. Petey sat in the chair, put the .357 on his lap, then waited.

It was dark when he heard keys jangling. The front door opened and two figures entered. One reached for the lamp near the door then switched it on.

"Surprise," Petey slurred.

Lucy looked at Petey then screamed. Her old man pushed her aside and drew a pistol from his pocket. He didn't hesitate; the small caliber weapon barked three times, each bullet hitting Petey square in the chest. Petey gazed at the holes and the dark liquid oozing from his torso. He looked up and grinned.

"My turn."

Petey blasted Lucy's old man with the .357. Two rounds hit him in the mouth, the third in his forehead. The man was dead before he hit the ground. Petey struggled to stand then walked stiffly to the door. Lucy had screamed herself hoarse, her terrified eyes locked on Petey.

"I must look a mess," Petey said. "But you safe now. I always keep my promises."

Petey left the house. Xavier met him halfway down the driveway. He grabbed Petey's arm and pulled him along.

"We got to go!" he said. They were almost to the car when something told Petey to turn around. Lucy stood in the doorway. The fear in her eyes was gone, replaced by confusion.

"Petey?" she said.

Petey nodded, then climbed into the car.

"Where to?" Xavier asked.

"The cemetery," Petey replied.

Xavier sped back to the graveyard. Petey got out of the car then stumbled back to his grave site. He was tired, so tired. He sat at the edge of the open hole.

"You want me to wait and cover you back up when you gone?" Xavier asked.

"Naw," Petey replied. "Let them find me just like this. Folks gonna be looking for who killed Lucy's old man. Those who know what he was doing to her are gonna think she did it."

"We can't let them think that," Xavier said.

"No we can't," Petey replied. "That's why I want you to go back and tell them the truth."

Xavier looked confused. "Tell them what?"

Petey grinned and a tooth fell from his mouth. "You tell them Petey came back."

Fallow

The troubles began at the end of winter. The snow, the source of the spring surge that filled the Uchee River and overflowed its banks, had been light that year, barely dusting the peaks of the Ocmulgee mountains. The Farmer and his family stayed snug in their modest home, feeding off smoked meats and preserves from the prior year. If there were no floods his land along the riverbank would not be fertile enough for planting for the coming season.

The situation worsened with the arrival of spring. The western rains did not appear in their normal abundance, leaving the high fields too dry. But still he planted and prayed, hoping the rain would come in time for the growing season. For a time there was expectation. Healthy sprouts emerged, promising a good season. Although the harvest would not be what he hoped, it would be enough.

That hope was crushed when the summer drought began. The crops withered in the fields under the brutal heat. He was forced to harvest early and plow what was ruined back into the dry soil. It was then the Farmer knew it would not be enough.

So, he sat on his porch in early fall, his shotgun resting in his lap as he patted his old hound dog Rufus on the head. His family hid in the woods beyond the dead cornfield, ready to flee if things turned toward the worse. He sat up when he heard the rumbling engines of the heavy trucks that always arrived this time of year. The Nomads were coming for his Portion and he did not have it. He lifted his shotgun, checking it one more time. There were three shells in the magazine, another ten in his vest pocket. Like the harvest, it wasn't enough. As the trucks came into view on the dusty road leading to his house, he stood.

"You ready, Rufus?" he said.

The old dog licked his hand then looked at him with rueful eyes.

The Farmer grinned. "I hear you."

The trucks stopped in front of his house. The doors swung open and four people emerged wearing heavy jackets, canvas pants and boots, their faces covered by thick scarves that rested on their shoulders. Each of them carried automatic rifles. From the rear of the second truck voices drifted, words of reassurance being spoken to calm those whose sobbing caused The Farmer's hands to instinctively tighten around his shotgun. One of the Nomads approached him, walking to the edge of his stairs.

"That's close enough," The Farmer said.

The Nomad halted, lowered the rifle then pulled down the face scarf, revealing the hard face of a middle age woman.

"Where's your Portion," she asked.

"In the shed out back," The Farmer replied.

The Nomad motioned with her head. As The Farmer moved toward the stairs Rufus jumped to his paws, growling as he bared his teeth. The Nomad took aim at the dog.

"Down, boy!" The Farmer shouted.

Rufus sat, still showing his teeth. The Nomad kept her gun trained on the dog.

"Did you come to kill a dog or did you come to get your Portion?" The Farmer said.

"Meat is meat," the Nomad replied.

The Farmer climbed down the stairs then sauntered around the back of his home to the shed. He heard the trucks rev up and follow him. He unlocked the shed then opened the wide doors as the Nomads approached. They brushed by him then marched into the shed. In moment they returned, their arms filled with his hard-earned harvest. Three trips they took before it was all gone.

The Nomad stood before him.

"Not much," she said. "We hear you're supposed to be the best."

"Hard season," The Farmer replied.

The woman spit at his feet. "Where's your family?"

The Farmer's eyes met the Nomad's.

"Like I said, hard season."

The Nomad smirked. She looked at his shotgun. She knew he was lying. "We left enough. We expect more next year."

The Nomads climbed into their trucks then drove away. Rufus jumped from the porch, barking and chasing the vehicles down the road. As they turned onto the main road, the canvas on the rear truck opened. Faces appeared, faces filled with fear and desperation. The Farmer looked away. There was nothing he could do for them. He waited until he was sure the trucks were far away before firing one shot into the air. His family would hear that shot then come out of hiding. He went inside his home to the old ham radio which shared a table with the sewing machine. He cranked the charger until he had enough power then radioed The Elder.

"Yes, Farmer?" The Elder spoke with a voice burdened by wisdom and time.

"We need to meet," The Farmer said. "Next year may be no better than this year."

"I'll gather the others," The Elder said. "We'll meet at First Oak. You sure you want to do this? We could reach out to the Citizens."

"They're no better," The Farmer said. "Everyone wants something for nothing. We need to handle this ourselves. We'll meet at First Oak. Tomorrow."

The Farmer exited his back door, striding across his barren field to the woods. His Wife and Daughter emerged from the brush, both draped in heavy camouflage jackets, his daughter tucked under his Wife's protective grip. In her right hand she held the handgun. She put the gun in her jacket pocket, the stoic look on her face giving way to relief. They embraced; a family hug that was too short lived.

"They're gone," he said.

"For now," she replied.

"They took too much," he said.

"We have more stashed in the caves."

"I don't know if it's enough."

The Farmer reached down then lifted his daughter into his arms. He looked into her fearful eyes and knew what had to be done.

"Will the bad men come back?" she asked.

"No," The Farmer replied. "The bad men won't come back. Daddy is going to make sure of it."

The Farmer's Wife looked at him skeptically and he shook his head. Once they were in the house, he carried his daughter to her room then tucked her in bed.

"Get some rest, little bird," he said. "Mommy and I are going to lay down, too."

"Okay, big bird," she said. She held his cheeks with her small hands then kissed his nose.

His Wife waited for him as he left the room.

"You shouldn't tell her things that aren't true," she said. "The Nomads will be back."

"I didn't lie," The Farmer replied. "I called the Elder."

The Wife's eyes widened. The Farmer handed his shotgun to his Wife then took the handgun from her.

"I should be back by midnight," he said. "If I'm not, take her and go to the caves. Stay there until someone comes for you."

The Farmer and his Wife kissed for a long time, like they used to when they were young. They held each other for a moment longer then let go. The Farmer went to his shed. As he reached the building Rufus met him, the old hound dog panting hard.

"You can't go with me," the Farmer said. "Get on that porch and keep an eye out. I'll be back at sundown."

He patted the dog on its head and it licked his hand before ambling off to the front porch. The Farmer climbed into his truck. It started with a loud bang and belched a cloud of white smoke before settling into a steady idle. He backed the truck out of the shed then stopped to climb out and close the shed door. Climbing back into the truck, he drove down the road to Meeting Tree.

He was not the first to arrive. Blacksmith's truck was there, as was Potter's and Beekeeper's. He could see the Meeting Tree's canopy towering over the other trees, its branches shedding its leaves as the tree crept toward a winter's sleep. As he trudged down the narrow path, he heard other trucks pulling up and doors slamming. The others gathered around him; they nodded and shook hands. There was little talk; everyone saving their words for what was about to take place.

They reached the tree. The massive white oak dwarfed the men and women sitting in a half circle under its branches. Resting before the trunk, flanked by her great-great-great grandchildren was The Elder. She seemed frail wrapped in her familiar woolen blanket, her wrinkled face resembling a land with many rivers. A small knit cap covered her head, strands of gray hair extending from beneath it.

"I'm glad you all have come," she said, her voice resonating across the clearing. "The Nomads came and they took too much. If they come again, we will starve. But if we don't give what we have to them, they will attack us, keep the weak, sell the strong and kill the useless. There is Unbalance."

The Farmer nodded with the others. He knew what would come next, words that had not been uttered under the Meeting Tree in centuries, words than none but the Elder had heard beyond bedtime stories.

The Elder gazed at each of those gathered with a certainty that belied her age.

"We must reclaim the Balance, for without it, both Farmers and Nomads will perish. One cannot exist without the other, but all must be equal. There must be a Summoning."

The murmurs under the tree were fearful and tense, yet no one protested. They had all seen the last truck. Someone had lost their family but would not speak up because of shame.

"We will draw straws to decide," she said.

The Farmer stepped forward.

"There is no need," he said. "I will do it."

Shock and dismay swept through the gathering like a fire through dry season grass.

"No," the Elder said. "You are the strongest."

"Which is why I should be the one," he replied.

The Elder looked at The Farmer a moment longer. There was sadness in her eyes, yet he knew she understood.

"So be it," she finally said. "Return in three days. I will be ready. I hope you will."

The Farmer nodded.

When the Farmer returned home his Wife and Daughter were fast asleep. He undressed then washed up, deciding not to shower because it would disturb his Wife. Afterwards he sat before the fireplace, the embers still glowing from the earlier fire. He watched the radiant specks rise with the updraft then disappear as they cooled. After a few more minutes he went to the room then climbed into bed as quietly as possible. No sooner did he lay his head on the pillow did his Wife speak.

"Who did they choose?" she asked.

"Me," he replied.

"They did not choose you," she said. "You volunteered."

The Farmer said nothing.

Her arms wrapped around his body, her hands pulling him closer she snuggled against his back. He felt her tears on the back of his neck and fought to hold back his own.

"How many days do you have?" she asked.

"Three."

They made love that night and every night until the time came for him to leave. That day he spent with his daughter, playing in the fields and the nearby woods. He listened to her ramblings as if she was a skilled djele, her voice so full of wonder and innocence. If there was any doubt of doing what he had to do, it was erased at that moment. He would not let them have his family. He would not let them die.

That night he tucked her in and read her a story. Once she was fast asleep, he went to the bedroom and changed clothes. His Wife watched; her arms folded tight about her body.

"You should wait until morning," she said.

"I told them I would come tonight," he said. "Night is best."

His wife came to him then hugged him.

"Please," she said. "Don't go tonight."

"If I don't go now, I won't go at all," he replied.

They kissed, then he pushed her away.

"Goodbye," he said. "Never let her forget me. When she is older, tell her why I did this."

The Farmer left his house. Rufus trotted to his side.

"Stay, boy," he said.

Rufus ignored him, keeping pace with him as he walked down the road toward the woods in the fading light. It was almost midnight when he reached the Meeting Tree. The Elder waited, standing before a blazing bonfire that functioned as a beacon and helped him find his way.

"You came," she said. "I was not sure you would."

"I am a man of my word," he said.

"Which is why it had to be you. I'm sorry."

The Farmer took off his shirt, dropping it on the ground beside him. He sat as he took off his shoes and socks, then unbuckled his belt. He tossed his belt aside then took off his pants and underwear. The Farmer took a deep breath, dropped to his knees, then closed his eyes.

"Let's get on with it," he said.

The Elder knelt before him, holding an old gourd in her trembling hands.

"Open your mouth," she commanded.

The Farmer did as he was told, and the Elder poured the elixir in his mouth. He expected it to be bitter, but it was slightly sweet and cool. He opened his eyes and the Elder handed him the gourd.

"Drink all of it," she said.

She stood and began walking away.

"How long will it take?" the Farmer asked.

"Not long," the Elder replied.

"Tell my family I love them," he said. He raised the gourd to his lips then drank the rest. The liquid settled in his stomach, transforming from cool to warm. The Farmer sweated despite the cool night against his exposed skin. Soon his stomach burned as if he had swallowed fire. He tried to remain calm, but the scream that burst from inside exposed his pain. He rolled in the high grass trying to quench the fire that consumed every inch of his body. He felt himself expanding, like a container about to burst. Hair sprouted from his skin, thick and coarse. His nails on his feet and hands peeled back then fell away, replaced by long claws. His mouth filled with sharp teeth, pushing his face forward into a long snout. The scream became a howl that ripped through the night air.

The thing that was once the Farmer stood on two legs. Its slitted pupils widened into black orbs that sucked in what little light the night shared. It sniffed, recognizing a scent that brought anger to it. That scent belonged to something it wanted to tear apart.

Another odor overtook the first, one that calmed it. It turned to see a small being standing before it. It looked into the being's eyes and felt complacent.

"Who are you?" the being said.

The thing that was the Farmer did not understand.

"WHO ARE YOU?" the being shouted.

The words cut through their thoughts, reaching a deeper consciousness.

"I am…the Farmer."

The being he recognized as the Elder smiled.

"I am the Elder. Hold on to who you are," she said. "And when this is done, you might be able to return to us." The Elder's expression became hard. "Now you must hunt," she said. "Restore the balance."

The Farmer faded back into the darkness, the creature taking his place. The scent that drove him mad with hate overwhelmed him and he ran through the night, seeking its source. He found it hours later, rising from a camp at a river's edge. The beast did not hesitate. It ran into the camp, tearing the others apart with its claws and teeth, caring not what it killed. The screams and shouts angered it more and it continued its rampage, ignoring the sharp pains throughout its body. It did not stop until the camp fell silent. But the stench persisted. It searched the camp until it found a survivor. The being recognized the face and it fell away, replaced by the Farmer. The farmer grabbed the woman by her bloodied shirt then pulled him to his feet.

"Tell them," he growled, 'that I protect mine. For every one of us taken, ten of you will die. Keep the Balance."

He dropped the woman on the ground then watched as she fled into the darkness. He was about to walk away when he heard voices, sounds of those he came to protect. He tracked the sounds to a metal box with a locked door. With the swipe of his hand, he broke the lock. The people inside screamed upon the sight of him and he stepped away.

"Do not be afraid," he said as soothing as he could. "You are free. Wait here until morning, then go home to your loved ones."

The thing that was the Farmer turned away from the others, picking up the scent of hate. The thing it freed would not do what it was told. It would return with others. It howled again, then loped into the darkness in pursuit. The being would lead it to the others, so it could finish what it was summoned to do. It would not stop until its loved ones were safe. It would continue until the fields were fallow again.

The Look

"So, you'll see her?"

Steve leaned backed in his leather executive chair, Pierre sitting on the opposite side of his desk. Pierre's eyes were wide like they always were when he was excited. He looked like a guppy. Steve flipped through the images on the flash drive Pierre had given him. The girl was attractive, but so were a million others. What he sought was The Look.

"I don't see it," he finally said.

Pierre leaned toward him. "That damn Tony! He's a crackpot photographer. I tell you, Steve, she's the girl you're looking for, the face of the new millennia. She has a . . . a . . . damn! I can't describe it. You'll have to meet her to see what I'm talking about."

When Steve looked up Pierre's animated expression had vanished. His heavy eyebrows were drawn in, his mouth barren of the familiar upward curve. Steve couldn't be sure but it looked like Pierre was getting serious.

"I'm giving a party this weekend at the lodge. Why don't you come? She'll be there, among others."

"Hell, I don't know, Pierre." But he did know. Among others meant escorts. Pierre had access to some of the best in Atlanta, mainly because he launched their careers. Besides, it had been a long time since he had his hand on some young flesh. There was the matter of the business weekend with Kristen, but he could handle that.

"I guess I can make it," he finally said. "But no promises."

Pierre's face gleamed. "Excellent! I guarantee you Steve, you'll love her!"

"Yeah, tell me about it. Now get out of here. I got a lot of work to finish."

Pierre strode out with a victorious swagger. Steve watched him leave and then thumbed through the photos again. The man always showed up in the middle of the night, interrupting the only time Steve had for paperwork. He was a short, fat, obnoxious coke head, but he did have an eye for women. But this girl didn't fit his type. She was a little thin and the dreadlocks did nothing for her. She did look good in an evening gown. Good, but not stunning. Positively not the Look for which he was searching. Still, if Pierre was so worked up over her it was worth taking a look.

He glanced at the mirrored clock resting on the opposite wall just out of reach of the ficus tree. One a.m. If he hurried, he could catch the last set at Marley's. He logged out of the photo file and got off the computer. Pierre's dream girl would have until the weekend.

* * *

Fall had come to North Georgia with its usual colorful brilliance, prompting the annual invasion of the Blue Ridge Mountains by thousands of urban Atlantans. A cleansing chill hung in the air but it was still warm enough to drive with the top down. Steve took the jeep for just that reason. He enjoyed the changing seasons; the emerging yellows and oranges broke the monotonous green of summer, just like the grey hairs intruding on his curly black mane. The hue, though premature, gave him a dignified look. It helped when dealing with young women. They needed a father image and he was happy to oblige if it meant signing the good ones. He glanced at Kristen sitting beside him in her trademark sweatshirt and blue jeans. A wide brim cowboy hat protected her raven hair from the wind. If it wasn't for the broad frown on her face Steve would have thought she was enjoying herself.

"Why do I have to go?" she whined.

"Because I have to," Steve replied. "Besides, we might see someone worth taking pictures."

Kristen laughed. "Yeah, right. I didn't know you were working for Only Models."

"Look, Pierre has this new girl he's really mad about." Steve reached over to the glove compartment and extracted the folder. "He said Tony took bad photos and I had to see her myself."

Kristen flipped through the photos.

"He's right."

"About the girl?"

"No, about Tony. These are some shitty photos."

Their free-wheeling cruise ended abruptly at the Cleveland city limits. Traffic was bumper to bumper through the town. They inched ahead, trapped in the exodus northward. By the time they reached Helen it was sunset. They stopped in the fake German village long enough to put up the top and get a quick lunch before continuing north into the mountains.

Pierre's retreat lay twenty miles further. Steve took advantage of the clear road, pressing down on the accelerator as he weaved through the forest on the winding roads. His reckless driving terrified Kristen, which amused him. He felt warm despite the cool night, eagerly anticipating what delights he might find at the party. He'd deal with the mystery woman as fast as possible then get to some real fun. He glimpsed at Kristen bouncing off the seat to the rhythm of Bob Marley. The only woman safe around him, he thought. She was appealing in an androgynous way, but not his type. His preference lay ahead.

The jeep made the transition from smooth pavement to rough dirt with a jolt, bright lights on and four-wheel drive kicked in. The lodge appeared ten minutes later, a stucco and wood trimmed replica of a German retreat bathed in yellow light.

"Hansel and Gretel could've found this place blind," Kristen said as she put on her shades. "I wonder what kind of candy we'll discover inside?"

Steve swerved the jeep into the first empty parking space. "They'll be something for everyone. Pierre's cool."

"Watch out for the witch!" Kristen crinkled her face and bent her fingers into claws.

As soon as he stepped out of the jeep, he was convinced the party was an elaborate sales pitch. Most of the parked cars he recognized and the heavy thumb of reggae bleeding out of the lodge was definitely his style. Pierre was going all out for this chick, but why? Love was the only reason he could come up with and that made him laugh. He pictured Pierre's fat ass waiting on Miss Haystack hand and foot, a too small waiter's uniform squeezing the blood out of him. Pierre should know better. Get involved, profits fall. The women were merchandise. The only ones you touched were the ones that wouldn't make the cut.

They climbed the wooden stairs and Kristen banged impatiently on the door. Pierre answered, his eyes shifting from wary to joyful when he recognized them.

"Steve! Kristen!" He grabbed their arms and pulled them inside. "Look everyone! Look who's here!"

From the raised foyer they surveyed the great room below. The fireplace on the opposite wall blazed and beside it the Ire-ites, the house band from Steve's favorite reggae club, added an island cadence to the flickering flames. Most of the people glanced up and waved.

Pierre took Steve's jacket. "If you had not shown up, this party would have been a disaster."

"I don't know," Steve replied. "Looks pretty good to me." His eyes wandered over the revelers, mentally separating the paid company from the guests. He spotted a couple of girl-friends on hold and gave them a friendly wink. He could have them if he wanted, but he didn't feel like romance.

Kristen laid a heavy hand on Pierre's shoulder. "Pete! What you got for the nose?"

Pierre frowned. "Go to the guest house out back."

"Great!" Kristen planted a wet kiss on Pierre's cheek and winked at Steve. "I'll be back when the party starts. Later!"

Pierre snatched out a handkerchief, scrubbing his jaw. "Why did you bring that coke head with you?"

"She's good company." Steve headed for the stairs; Pierre followed. "I also needed someone to take a few shots if this dream girl of yours turns out to be anything. Is she here?"

"She's still dressing," Pierre answered. "I tell you Steve, you won't be disappointed. She's magnificent!"

They descended into the crowd, Steve nod-ding, shaking, and grinning his way to the band. He picked up a tall red head along the way and they cleared a space on the floor with their vigor-ous dancing. Other couples joined in; soon the great room undulated with bodies rapt with the Caribbean beat. *Now this is a party*, Steve thought. The drinks and drugs could wait. There was nothing better than attractive bodies moving to a good beat, creating a glimpse of later pas-sion.

The band slowed the pace after the fourth song. Steve had a dark brown beauty before him named Tanya. They followed the lead, pulling each other close. He was closing his eyes, savoring Tanya's sweet smell when he felt someone staring at him. He cracked his eyes, looking over Tanya's shoulder for the culprit. A few couples danced while others mingled around the snack table. No one seemed interested in him. He was about to dismiss it to paranoia when the feeling swept over him again. His legs buckled and he almost fell. Luckily, Tanya was stronger than she appeared.

"Watch it, love," she said. 'Too much toot will do it every time."

"Sorry." Steve turned about, looking to the direction he sensed was right. Pierre stood in the foyer, eyes wide and twinkling. Beside him posed the other reason the evening had been planned. She was a foot and a half taller than her mentor. Black dreadlocks twisted down to her shoulders, flanking a golden-brown face. She was full-figured and finely shaped. The matching halter and wrap-around skirt she wore was an excellent choice. The island nymph, obviously Pierre's idea. He was playing to Steve's every weakness. But it was her eyes that trapped Steve's attention, deep brown orbs that seemed ancient yet innocent. He excused himself from Tanya and made his way to the pair.

Pierre rustled like a proud father. "Steven McCarthy, I'd like you to meet Ms. Kyla Swane."

Steve took her extended hand anxiously. "Ms. Swane. May I call you Kyla?"

"Of course, Mr. McCarthy. A man of your reputation needn't ask."

"Call me Steve, please." Her hand felt eerie, cold yet compelling. He wanted to hold more than just an appendage. He needed more.

Pierre's piping voice cut into his musing. "What did I tell you? Isn't she magnificent?"

Kyla blushed. "Pierre, you're embarrassing me!"

"No, he's not," Steve said. "The photos I saw don't do you justice. There's something about you that eludes the camera. Your eyes..."

"What about my eyes, Steven?"

Steve hurtled back in time, images of decades past flashing by in an accelerated parade. In every sequence Kyla was the only permanence, unchanging and ever beautiful. He swayed and grabbed the railing for support.

"Are you alright?" Pierre asked.

Steve steadied himself, his eyes still engaged with Kyla's. The sensation that held him was tempered by a twinge of foreboding.

"I'm fine," he finally said. "Excuse me, I need to find Kristen."

Steve exploded from the front door and stumbled down the stairs. His breath came in gasps, his head throbbed and his heart pounded relentlessly against his chest. Easing himself down on the last stairs, he took a deep breath to regain control. This was ridiculous, he thought. He felt childish, like a boy meeting his secret love for the first time. Another part of him responded to something intangible, an unsettling feeling that welled up from deep inside.

"Can't handle it, huh?"

Steve jerked his head up to see Kristen standing in front of him, her hands deep in her pockets.

"I was looking for you," Steve said. "Get your camera. I want shots of Pierre's wonder woman."

"So, you met her?"

Steve felt a warm rush through his body. "Yes, I did. Pierre's pictures are trash. I'm still not quite sure if she has what I want though."

"What's there to be sure of?" Kristen said. "Either it's there or it's not."

"It's not that simple this time. Go on and get the gear."

Steve waited outside for Kristen. With her he would have more control and be able to keep his mind on business. Kristen returned with her cameras and tripod.

"Okay, Sugar Daddy, let's do this," Kristen said, sauntering past him to climb the stairs.

"I hate it when you call me that," Steve said as he followed.

Kristen laughed. "Truth hurts."

The band was taking a break as they entered. Steve spotted Pierre working the room with Kyla by his side, the man loud and energetic, Kyla restrained but no less enchanting.

"There she is," he said. "Her name is Kyla."

"She is a looker," Kristen said. "Somebody should break Tony's cameras and kick his ass."

They pushed through the crowd to the duo. Steve placed a hand on Kyla's shoulder and she turned to him with a smile.

"You're back!" She noticed Kristen and shared a smile with her as well. Kristen smiled back and took pictures.

Pierre clapped his hands. You're taking pictures! Outstanding!"

Steve nodded, fearing his voice might crack if he spoke. He watched Kyla move with the camera with an assurance beyond her experience. She gazed at him between shots, her penetrating eyes pulling forth feelings from him he tried desperately to hide.

The band started again and the crowd flowed back to the dance floor. Steve found himself standing face to face with Kyla.

"Dance?" she asked.

He nodded. She took his hand and guided him to the floor. She was an excellent dancer, prancing around him with skillful gracefulness.

"No fair!" he complained. "You're a pro."

"Professionals get paid," Kyla replied. "I only dance like this when I'm inspired."

As they danced Steve realized he'd been falling in love since the moment they met. The awareness amazed and frightened him.

"Have you seen the house?" Kyla asked.

Her question broke his musing.

"A few times," he replied. "Pierre lets me crash here when I'm trout fishing in the area."

"Oh. What about the guest house?"

Steve wanted to lie but he couldn't. Those endless eyes demanded the truth.

"No, I haven't."

"Come on!" She grabbed his hand with surprising strength and towed him across the great room. Kristen appeared from nowhere and took a few pictures. "Bingo!" she said.

Kyla glared at Kristen. "No more pictures."

Kristen stiffened. She lowered the camera then walked away. Steve bristled.

"Hey, you don't . . ."

Kyla looked into his eyes. "We don't need her anymore." She pulled him toward the door. Steve shook his head as an unexplained terror gripped him. They ran out the back door down the stone walkway winding to the guest house. Kyla had overwhelmed his mind and was overpowering his body. He tried to pry his hand free but her thin fingers refused to give.

"Kyla, what the hell is going on?"

"You'll find out soon." She looked back at him and smiled. "Don't worry, it'll be fun."

He stopped resisting. The guest house was quaint, a white stained wood farmhouse structure with dark cedar trimmed exterior. Kyla opened the front door and led him inside. The aroma of apple cinnamon struggled to mask a strange musk filling the cottage. The room they entered was sparsely furnished, a pit group and mirrored coffee table its only inhabitants. Someone had started a fire, the smell of hickory adding to the comforting mood.

"Don't be afraid," she said. Her voice lost its innocuous tone, becoming as archaic as her eyes. "I won't hurt you."

Steve jerked his hand free then stumbled away. He grabbed his head and shook it violently, trying to bring order to his feelings. A tempest churned inside him; on the surface desire reigned but below instinct warned him.

"Kyla, I don't think this is a good idea," he managed to say.

She undid her halter, took it off and let it float to the floor. The fear inside him floundered then drowned in a torrent of lust. He staggered to her as she took off her wraparound skirt. Steve took off his clothes and they fell to the carpeted floor, the flames outlining their bodies, their arms entangled about each other like vines, kisses like embers smattering his cheeks, eyes, lips, and throat.

This was too much, too soon. He yelled and tried to break away. Kyla pinned his arms, refusing to let him stand. She raised her head and this time he saw the fangs glinting from the firelight, pointed pearls meant only for him. As she plunged for his throat calmness returned to his frayed mind. He had been right all along. It wasn't The Look. It was more.

Battle Axe

He's a battle axe,
In the time of a war
He's a battle axe,
In the time of a war
He's a battle axe,
In the time of a war
Shelter in the time of a storm

Abraham listened to the singing seeping out the doors of Piney Grove AME Zion Church with his eyes closed, the power of each word warming his body. After buttoning the collar of his overcoat, he gripped his walking staff with his right hand, lifted his large suitcase with his left hand, and ambled toward the church entrance. He liked the old churches, buildings constructed over a hundred years ago by the weary hands of the ancestors of the people that now attended. He imagined just about every person sitting on the worn pews inside were related to those founders and each other in some way. It was just what he was looking for, and just what he needed. A shelter in the time of a storm.

By the time he reached the front doors of the church, the choir had finished their song and the pastor had taken his place behind the pulpit. Abraham closed his eyes, listening to him pray before the sermon. He had a young, strong voice, the kind that stirred emotions in the congregation but lacked the experience to make his words sit in your soul. In another couple of decades or so he would. If he was still preaching.

After prayer, the pastor directed the parishioners to the book and chapter that served as the inspiration of the day's word. Abraham grinned, mouthing the words with the pastor. Abraham knew the King James Version of the Bible by heart. He also memorized the Ethiopian Bible, as well as the Coptic Version. There were more, many more, but these were the ones that were special to him. Ethiopia was his heart and home, but it had been a long time since his eyes beheld her beauty. He would return one day, but not yet.

Abraham continued to wait outside until the doors of the church were opened and the pastor put out the call for new members. Applause rose twice, which meant two new souls had become members. After a joyful welcome from the congregation, the call for tithes went out. Abraham opened the doors and entered.

Everyone's eyes immediately fell on him. A stranger in a small town will never go unnoticed, and Abraham's appearance most likely garnered extra attention. His worn clothes and old shoes were still dusty from the road and sweat beaded on his bald head. His black skin stood in stark contrast to the various brown hues of the members, and his height could not be ignored.

Abraham set down his suitcase then ambled up the aisle to make an offering. The deacons shook his hand limply as he made his way forward. He reached into his pants pocket and took out a solid gold coin. As he dropped it into the sweetgrass basket, he looked at the pastor. The man was young, but he knew what that coin meant. Abraham smirked, made his way back to the rear of the church then waited for the benediction.

The members trailed out slowly, taking the time to catch up with each other and share the latest gossip. They greeted Abraham kindly as people in such places do, careful to hide their curiosity. The children were not so modest.

"Who that man, mama?"
"Why is he so tall and so black?"
"Daddy, that man ain't got no hair!"
"Why he walking with that stick? Is he crippled?"

The pastor finally said farewell to the last member. He locked his eyes with Abraham, then strode up to him. His voice was not kind.

"What are you doing here?"

Abraham smiled. "If you know who I am, then you know why I'm here."

"That's impossible! We're God fearing people in these parts. I know every last one of my members like family. If there was something wrong, I would know!"

Abraham sighed. It always started the same way.

"Pastor Long, I'm sure you think you know them. But everybody has secrets. Besides, not everyone in this county is part of your flock." The pastor glared at Abraham. "How do you know my name?"

Abraham's stomach growled. It had been a while since he had a good meal.

"We can talk about that later. What I need right now is a good meal and a bit of rest."

Pastor Long hesitated before answering. "There's a motel a mile down the road. Sarah Birdsong is the owner. The rates are reasonable and the food is good. Tell her I sent you."

"I was expecting you to invite me into your home," Abraham said.

"I'll do no such thing," Long replied. "I'll meet you at the motel."

Abraham shrugged. Pastor Long was going to be difficult.

"As you wish. But you need to get your head right. This situation has to be handled. The longer we wait, the worse it will get. Do you understand?"

Pastor Long swallowed. "I do."

Abraham extended his hand and Pastor Long took it. The young man had a firm grip, which pleased Abraham. He might just be strong enough to survive what was to come.

"Which way is the motel?"

Long hesitated before answering. "I'll take you. Give me a minute to close up."

Abraham smiled. "I'm in no hurry."

The pastor walked back to his church, entering the front door then closing it behind him. Abraham took the time to feel the area around him, extending his senses across the dormant fields into the surrounding woods. This was his first time in the Deep South. He could feel the spirits of this land, both good and evil. Though the landscape, flora, and fauna were unique, the people were the same as others around the world. Customs and costumes were different, but emotions were always similar.

Pastor Long pulled up a few minutes later in his pickup truck. Abraham put his suitcase in the truck bed, climbed into the passenger side and they were on their way.

"You have a robust congregation," he said.

"Folks this way ain't got nothing much except their faith," Long replied. "Praying is the only hope they have."

"You from here?"

Long shook his head. "I'm from up the road. Macon."

Abraham recalled the city. "So you're a city boy. Why would someone like you settle in a town like this?"

"I needed the quiet," Long replied.

"War can do that to a person."

Long glanced at Abraham. "How you know I served?"

"I know a lot about you, Percy Long. That's why I came to your church. You're a person that knows violence. I might need that."

Percy pulled the truck to the roadside.

"Look priest, I know what kind of man you are, and I respect you for what you do. Takes a person of real faith to make that kind of sacrifice. But I'm not your man. Now Reverend Thomas, he's the kind of man you're looking for. That man's faith is deep like oak roots."

"Randolph Thomas's faith is strong, but he's old."

"Y'all look about the same age if you ask me."

"We're not. I'm older. Much older."

Percy looked confused for a moment. He shook his head then pulled back onto the road. "I'll do what I can, but I can't get directly involved. I'm responsible for these people's families and their spirits."

"If I can't do what I came here to do, they won't have either. So if you really want to protect them, you'll be there when I need you."

Pastor Long took a left turn at a four-way stop and continued on. They finally arrived at the motel, a single row of rooms with a gravel parking lot. The check-in area occupied a separate building, crowned with a sign that read simply, 'Motel.' As the pastor pulled into parking, a stout woman with dark brown skin exited the main building wearing a long dress covered by a soiled apron. A flowered scarf covered her head, a few strands of hair escaping the edge. She wiped her hands with a plaid cloth.

"Afternoon, pastor," she said. "What brings you 'round here? Looking for another lost sheep?"

"Hey Sarah. Not this time. Brought you some business."

The slight smile on Sarah's face disappeared as she looked Abraham up and down. Abraham walked up to Sarah and extended his hand.

"My name's Abraham. It's nice to meet you."

"Man's lying already," Sarah replied.

"Come on, Sarah," Percy said. "Abraham here is a priest. A very special one."

"If you say so," Sarah replied. "Rooms are $25 a night standard, $35 if you're taking breakfast and dinner. I don't do lunch. How long you planning to stay?"

"I'm not sure," Abraham replied. "As long as it takes for me to do what I came to do."

Sarah tilted her head. "What's that supposed to mean?"

"A week," Abraham replied. "Maybe two."

"I need a week's pay up front, the rest when you check out."

Sarah put out her hand. Abraham reached into his coat pocket, pulled out his wallet, then paid Sarah, counting out the bills. Sarah nodded then took a room key out of her apron pocket.

"Room four. I'll bring you clean towels. Bed's already been made. Enjoy your stay."

"Miss Sarah, you wouldn't happen to have any leftovers from breakfast, would you? I'm mighty hungry."

"I do. Help yourself to what's left."

She turned then walked away.

"Friendly people in this county," Abraham said.

"That's just Sarah," Percy replied. "Maybe you should stay with me."

"I'll be fine," Abraham said. "Besides, unless you're married, I suspect her breakfast and dinner will be better than anything you can cook."

Percy laughed. "You're right about that. So when should I expect to see you again?"

"I don't know," Abraham replied. "But get ready and stay ready."

Sarah met him at the door of the main building with a brown bag. Abraham took it then shuffled to his room as Percy drove away. He opened the door and was relieved. It was a better than average space, with a decent sized bed, a dresser, a small desk with a chair, and a nightstand on which a small lamp rested. Abraham placed his suitcase beside the bed then inspected the bathroom before returning to the bed and taking off his coat. He ate the cold bacon and grits, then took a shower. The hot water didn't work, but he didn't mind. After the shower he ambled to his suitcase then took out a t-shirt and coveralls. Under the clothing were the tools of his trade: three old, worn bibles, an axe, a machete, a shotgun, and his favorite, his shotel. Abraham hummed as he sharpened the axe. He tested the edge with his finger, making a small cut on his thumb. Next was the machete, a souvenir from his time in Haiti. His smile faded as the memories came back. Haiti was grim work. Quite a few saints traveled home that day, but it was well worth it. As he put the blade back into its sheath, his eyes fell on the shotgun. This was a new addition, a gift after a cleansing in Louisiana. He broke the gun down, cleaning and oiling each part with Myron oil, careful not to overuse the rare and sacred liquid. He traveled far to obtain it; it was the most important part of his arsenal. Last to get his attention was the shotel. It was his most precious possession and his least used. He kept it for sentimental reasons, but its effectiveness was still relevant.

After cleaning his tools, took his Ethiopian Bible and sat at the old desk to read. The words comforted and grounded him in his purpose. He had no idea what he would face, but he was prepared for the outcome, whatever it would be.

* * *

Abraham greeted the morning sun in the motel parking lot. Eyes closed, he let his senses run free, seeking a destination. A foul taste touched the back of his throat and he coughed.

"North," he whispered.

The smell of fresh cooked bacon met him at the motel office door. Sarah carried pans from the kitchen, placing them side by side on a long table.

"We got grits, eggs, bacon and biscuits," she said without looking his way. "You can get two servings and then be on your way."

"Yes ma'am," Abraham replied.

"I ain't no ma'am, especially to you. You old as I am."

"Thank you, Sarah."

Sarah's cooking was as good as she was mean. Abraham ate his two servings with relish. When Sarah came for his plate, he gave her a hopeful look.

"Two servings," she said.

Abraham smirked then got up from the table.

"Where you headed?" Sarah called out.

"Thought I'd walk around, see if I could find some day work."

"Head south into town. Day laborers usually wait out in front of Bill Haney's store."

"Don't think I'll do that," Abraham replied. "I got a feeling where I can find it."

Sarah folded her arms across her chest. "How you got a feeling about somewhere you ain't never been?"

Abraham turned and smiled. "I was born that way."

Sarah walked away with Abraham's dishes.

"Crazy old man," she muttered. "Talking 'bout he got a feeling. I got a feeling he ain't gonna find a damn thing."

The sun rose, rolling its light and heat across the land like a worn quilt. Abraham ambled along the side of the road, catching wind gusts from passing cars and pickup trucks. Axe slung over his shoulder, he seemed to fit into a place where work was scarce for a man like him. Cars and trucks rolled by, the drivers and passengers sharing perfunctory smiles and waves.

Abraham was a few miles into his trek when a battered pickup truck slowed beside him. The driver was a heavyset white man, his thick arm hanging outside the door, the smile on his red sweaty face predatory. Five men sat in the bed of the truck, their unkempt clothes and solemn expressions a reflection of their situation. A sense of dread weighed heavily on Abraham; his grip tightening on his axe.

"You looking for work, boy?"

Abraham forced a smile to his face. "I am."

"Get in."

Abraham hesitated. The driver's eyes narrowed.

"What you waiting on? You want to get paid or what?

Abraham backed away from the truck.

"I appreciate the offer, but I think I'll just keep looking."

The truck driver grinned. "I thought you'd say that, demon killer."

The false laborers leaped out the truck bed, teeth bared and fingers transformed into claws. The driver transformed as well, his clothes replaced by coarse black hair, his face wolflike.

Abraham swung his axe, decapitating the first demon then dropped and backrolled away from the other. His axe sliced the abdomen of the second demon, releasing putrid guts that spilled onto his shoes. Abraham's swing missed the third demon; he winched as it bit his shoulder while the other demon grabbed his axe.

"Hold him!" the demon shouted.

The massive creature stomped to Abraham, slobber dripping from its maw.

"You thought you could come here unnoticed, priest?" it growled. "We smelled you the moment you entered our realm."

The beast leaned forward. "The only reason I don't kill you now is because our master wishes to do it himself."

Abraham smiled then bit off the demon's nose. It screamed as it staggered backwards, black bile seeping through its claws. Abraham yanked arms free from the stunned minions then snatched the vial of Myron oil from his pocket. He splashed the oil in the faces of both of them and they fell to their knees, their howls drowning out the other demon's wails. They melted, flesh and bones diminishing until all that remained was two smoking heaps.

Abraham picked up his axe then marched to the large demon. It crouched warily, its eyes darting from Abraham to the other dead monsters.

"You are no priest," it said.

"I am," Abraham replied, "and I'm not."

Abraham's pupils transformed from circles to slits, his fingers extending into claws. The large demon's face showed its fury.

"Traitor!"

It leapt at Abraham. Abraham waited until it was almost upon him before dropping to his knees and raising his axe. The razor sharp edge sliced the demon from its neck to its loins. It was dead before it hit the ground.

Abraham knelt beside the demon then took its head into his hands as he reverted to his human form. It had been a long time since he used his hive mind, and the sensation repelled him. After a few seconds, he found what he was looking for. He stood then applied a few drops the oil on the large demon. In seconds it melted into the ground like the others.

Abraham searched the truck. The keys were still in the ignition. He started the vehicle then drove back to the hotel. Time was of the essence. He rushed into his room to gather his things, throwing them into his suitcase.

"Who'd you steal that truck from?"

Abraham turned to see Sarah standing in the doorway. He grimaced as he finished packing.

"I ain't harboring no thieves!" she said. "Hard enough for a colored woman to own a business establishment then have to be dealing with miscreants. I need you to leave my hotel, Abraham."

"That's what I'm doing. I found what I was looking for."

Abraham brushed by Sarah as he left the room. She grabbed his wrist.

"Oh no you don't! You owe me for another week's rent."

"I only stayed one night. One week's pay should be enough."

"It's not."

Abraham looked down at Sarah's hand gripping his wrist, then looked into her eyes. His pupils transformed.

"Let go of me," he growled.

Sarah's eyes went wide and she jerked her hand away from Abraham as she grasped her chest.

"Lord Almighty!"

Abraham tossed his suitcase into the truck bed then climbed into the truck cabin and drove away. He watched Sarah from the rearview mirror as she recovered then ran to the office. Abraham rarely revealed himself, but sometimes people needed the Hell scared out of them. Sarah would either call the police and report a stolen truck, or she would cower in her room hoping he wouldn't come after her. Abraham didn't care. He had work to do, and he needed help doing it.

Abraham drove to the church. Percy's car was parked out front; he saw the young pastor tending the nearby cemetery. He hesitated at the sight of the sacred ground. There was a time he couldn't set foot in such a place, but that was long ago. He honked the truck horn; Percy looked up then strolled to the truck. His welcoming smile disappeared when he saw who was driving.

"Get in," Abraham said. "It's time."

Percy started for his car. "I have to get some things."

Abraham shook his head. "No you don't. I got everything we'll need. Now come on!"

Abraham climbed out of the driver's seat and gave Percy the keys.

"You drive."

"Where we going?"

"I don't know yet, but I have a feeling."

Percy drove the truck onto the main road.

"Which way?"

Abraham lowered his head then closed his eyes. "Right."

Percy sped down the two lane highway, casting glances at Abraham. The priest concentrated on the foul trail leading to the demon. They came to a four way stop.

"Left," Abraham said.

He opened his eyes as they drove by a fallow cornfield swarming with red-winged black birds. It was a huge flock, a thousand birds at least. As they continued down the road, the swarm came closer to the road. Abraham watched the birds, his eyes narrowing. A moment later, his eyes widened.

"Speed up," he said.

"Why?"

"Speed up! Now!"

Percy was about to protest when hundreds of blackbirds engulfed the pickup. Their small bodies crashed against the windows, their feathers and blood becoming a blinding shield. Percy began slowing down.

"What are you doing?" Abraham asked.

"I can't see! I can't keep driving."

"Don't stop, and don't slow down! I'll tell you what to do!"

Percy prayed then pressed the gas. Abraham grimaced as he focused on the spiritual spoor.

"Right!"

Percy jerked the wheel to the right. The bird swarm intensified, the front windshield cracking from the constant battering. Percy turned on the wipers out of desperation.

"Left!" Abraham shouted.

Percy turned left. The truck transitioned from paved street to gravel path, the truck jostled by the uneven surface.

"Speed up!" Abraham shouted.

"Are you crazy?!?"

Abraham pressed his left foot on top of Percy's, pushing the truck to maximum speed.

"This is too fast!" Percy protested. "We might . . ."

"Brace yourself!" Abraham said.

"What . . ."

The truck crashed. Percy and Abraham lurched forward, Percy's head hitting the steering wheel. Abraham hit the dashboard then bounced back into his seat. The truck engine died, the vehicle rolling forward on momentum then stopping. As the truck came to a halt, the swarming birds disappeared, revealing a dirt road leading to a large farm complex.

"We're here," Abraham said.

Abraham got out of the truck, stepping over and on bird carcasses as he walked to the truck bed. He let down the gate them climbed to the bed to retrieve his suitcase. Percy waited at the gate. Abraham opened the suitcase revealing his tools. He strapped his dagger around his waist, then gave Percy the other. He then grabbed his sword.

"What's that?" Percy asked.

"It's called a shotel," Abraham replied. "It's an old weapon. Particularly good for killing demons."

"So what do I get?" Percy replied. "And please don't give me a sword. You might as well kill me now."

Abraham admired Percy's ability to make humor in such a grave situation. He was a true warrior. He reached into the case and took out the shotgun.

"Here."

Percy smiled as he took the gum. He worked the pump a few times then aimed it.

"This has been well maintained," he said. "Where are the shells?"

Abraham reached into his pocket and took out one shell.

"That's it?" Percy said. "You got to be kidding me!"

"It's all you need. Your faith is enough. Trust me."

"I think I want a sword."

A piercing howl shattered their conversation. Abraham looked around the truck and spotted a demon horde running toward them.

"I'll take the lead. Keep them off me."

Abraham ran to face their attackers. Percy caught up with him, loading the one shell into the chamber. Abraham glanced back; Percy had his axe slid between his belt and his waist.

"Just in case you lied."

Abraham nodded then rushed forward. He raised his sword to kill the first demon, but there was a large boom and the creature's head exploded. A grim smile creased Abraham's bloodied face. Percy was committed.

The duo worked as a team, taking down the demons with sword and shot. Halfway through the slaughter, the demons realized the futility of their efforts. They tried to flee, but Abraham and Percy would not let them. Abraham was killing the last of them when something large and hard slammed into him. The shotel flew from his hand as he tumbled across the ground. His feet found purchase and he stood, shaking his head clear. Standing before him was the one he sought.

"Kakalum," the demon said.

"Baas," Abraham replied.

"So the stories are true," Baas said. "Not only have you betrayed us, but you have also taken their form."

"Repent or die," Abraham said.

Baas laughed. "There is no redemption for us. Me, nor you. You know the deal we made. You cannot break it on the word of one priest. Nothing will save your soul."

Abraham felt Baas's words. Doubt entered his mind for the first time in many years.

"Abraham, what is he talking about?" Percy asked.

Abraham turned to Percy, confusion on the pastor's face.

"Come back to us, Kakalum," Baas said. "We will join hands as brothers, and feast on this one's flesh."

"Like hell you will!"

Percy fired the shotgun. Baas dodged the shot as Abraham transformed into his true self and sprinted for his shotel with inhuman speed. As he picked it up and spun around, Baas appeared behind Percy, his mouth opened wide.

"Down!" Abraham shouted.

Percy dropped as Abraham threw his sword. Baas was fast, but not fast enough. The sword struck his shoulder, sending him spinning to the ground. Abraham ran over to Percy and snatched the axe from his belt. He stood over Baas as the beast struggled to take the sword from his shoulder.

"You might as well stop," Abraham said. "The Myron oil is doing its work."

"Bastard!" Baas screamed. "I'll see you in hell!"

Abraham brought the axe down on Baas' head. He smashed the weapon into the beast again and again until nothing was left but pieces. As he lowered the axe, he heard the cocking of the shotgun. He turned to see Percy aiming the gun at his head.

"Is what he said true?" Percy asked.

"Yes," Abraham replied.

"So you're a demon?"

"I am . . . I was. Centuries ago, in the land you know as Ethiopia, I gave up my soul to live. I did not know the price I would pay. I was consumed by what I had become, and I took it out on those I once cared for. No priest or person had the strength or faith to stand against me . . . except Abraham."

Abraham's mind traveled back to that day. "I nearly lost my life. Never had I encountered a human so strong, so determined, so full of faith. I felt remorse when I finally struck him down. As I stood over him watching him die, his face became solemn, peaceful. He looked into my eyes and said . . .

"I forgive you."

"And then he died."

Tears welled in Abraham's eyes. "This ordinary man had fought me and then given his life, embracing that which I had sold my soul to avoid. Those three words struck me harder than any weapon."

Abraham looked up. "It was then I assumed his name and his life and took up his calling, hoping that I would one day be forgiven by a higher calling."

Abraham looked at Percy, who still held the shotgun at his head.

"If you decide to kill me, then so be it. I am ready. All that I ask is that you consider continuing the task I accepted, and that you honor Abraham's memory." With that, Abraham closed his eyes.

"He called you Kakalum," Percy said.

Abraham nodded. "That was my name. I haven't been called that in centuries."

Percy's eyes went wide. "Centuries?"

Abraham grinned. "I told you I was older that I look."

Percy lowered the shotgun. "I'm not killing you," Percy said. "Not because you deserve to live, but because I have no intentions of become a demon hunter."

"You need to go," Abraham said. "The authorities will be here soon."

Percy extended the shotgun to Abraham but he shook his head.

"It is yours. You have the faith to use it."

Percy smiled. "The truck, too?"

"Of course. Now go. I have much to do."

Percy climbed into the truck. "Abraham . . . Kakalum, whoever you are, I hope you find what you're looking for."

Abraham smiled. "Thank you, pastor. Now go."

Percy drove away. Abraham took out his vial of Myron oil then dispersed drops on all the demon bodies. He walked up to the main house, inspecting it for any stragglers. Finding it empty, he located cans of kerosene and soaked the floors. With the light of a match, the building went up in flames.

Abraham retreated into the nearby woods. He inspected his suitcase, then looked at his Myron oil supply. He always wondered why it didn't damage him like the others. Maybe if was a show of some redemption. Whatever the reason, it was almost empty; he needed more. He would have to travel back to Ethiopia for it, which pleased him. It had been a while since he was home, decades to be exact. Maybe more than just oil awaited him there. He secured his suitcase then faded into the pines.

Milton J. Davis is an acclaimed Black speculative fiction author and the founder of MVmedia, LLC, a publishing company dedicated to producing science fiction, fantasy, and sword-and-soul narratives that highlight African and African Diaspora cultures. Based in Metro Atlanta, Davis has been a prominent figure in the Afrofuturist and Black speculative fiction communities for over two decades. In 2022, Davis was honored with the East Coast Black Age of Comics Convention Pioneer Lifetime Achievement Award, recognizing his significant contributions to Black speculative fiction. In 2024, he received the ConCarolinas Polaris Award, and the DeepSouth Con Phoenix Award for his contributions to Southern fandom.

For more books by Milton Davis and other Black Fantastic authors, visit MVmedia today!

www.mvmediaatl.com

MILTON J DAVIS